Paper Heart

Also by Cat Patrick

Tornado Brain

Just Like Fate, with Suzanne Young

The Originals

Revived

Forgotten

PAPER HEART

CAT PATRICK

DISCARDED
from Iowa City Public Library

G. P. Putnam's Sons

IOWA CITY

JUL -- 2021

PUBLIC LIBRARY

G. P. PUTNAM'S SONS

An imprint of Penguin Random House LLC, New York

Copyright © 2021 by Cat Patrick
Excerpt from *Tornado Brain* copyright © 2020 by Cat Patrick

Penguin supports copyright. Copyright fuels creativity, encourages diverse voices, promotes free speech, and creates a vibrant culture. Thank you for buying an authorized edition of this book and for complying with copyright laws by not reproducing, scanning, or distributing any part of it in any form without permission. You are supporting writers and allowing Penguin to continue to publish books for every reader.

G. P. Putnam's Sons is a registered trademark of Penguin Random House LLC.

Visit us online at penguinrandomhouse.com

Library of Congress Cataloging-in-Publication Data
Names: Patrick, Cat, author.
Title: Paper heart / Cat Patrick.
Description: New York: G. P. Putnam's Sons, [2021] | Summary: Companion to: Tornado brain.
Identifiers: LCCN 2020058377 (print) | LCCN 2020058378 (ebook) |
ISBN 9781984815347 (hardcover) | ISBN 9781984815354 (ebook)
Subjects: CYAC: Grief—Fiction. | Anxiety—Fiction. | Friendship—Fiction. | Art—Fiction. |
Day camps—Fiction. | Camps—Fiction. | Family life—Fiction.
Classification: LCC PZ7.P2746 Pap 2021 (print) | LCC PZ7.P2746 (ebook) | DDC [Fic]—dc23
LC record available at https://lccn.loc.gov/2020058377
LC ebook record available at https://lccn.loc.gov/2020058378

Manufactured in Canada
ISBN 9781984815347

10 9 8 7 6 5 4 3 2 1

Design by Eileen Savage | Text set in Alda OT

This book is a work of fiction. Any references to historical events, real people, or real places are used fictitiously. Other names, characters, places, and events are products of the author's imagination, and any resemblance to actual events or places or persons, living or dead, is entirely coincidental.

For my elf,
the one who lifts everyone else.
I've got you.

Paper Heart

prologue

"Shhh!" Frankie hissed in the darkness, which only made me and Colette giggle harder. "You guys are so annoying!"

In the furniture-packed bunk room, Frankie was on one of the top bunks; our cousin Kennedy was sleeping like a starfish on the full-size bed, her covers rumpled on the floor; and Colette and I shared the queen-size bed.

Colette and I had been telling ghost stories—quietly, I'd thought.

"Frankie, lower your voice," I whispered. "You're going to wake up Kennedy. That would be zero percent amazing."

"Whatever," Frankie said, still too loudly. She was sometimes not great at matching her volume to the situation. "You guys are zero percent amazing! You're making it impossible to sleep!" In the moonlight through the window, I saw her throw her arm over her eyes. "And the crickets are so loud! They're driving me crazy! I hate it here. I just want to go home. Wyoming sucks!"

She sounded like she was going to cry.

"We're sorry," I whispered, immediately feeling bad. She'd had a hard time falling asleep as it was. I sat up and inchwormed toward the bottom of the bed since I was on the side next to the wall. "Here, we'll go downstairs so you can sleep."

Kennedy rolled over with a sleep-groan. The rest of us held still like we'd been freeze-tagged until she got settled again.

I turned back to tell Colette, "Come on," but she was already out of the bed, ducking into her sweatshirt. A best friend to both me and Frankie since kindergarten, Colette knew how to disarm my twin sister almost as well as I did.

"Want my noise-canceling headphones?" she whispered to Frankie, resting her arms on the frame of the bunk. "They'll drown out the stupid crickets, at least."

Frankie thought about it, then said, quieter, "Fine."

"Sorry for keeping you up," I whispered, hovering in the doorway while Colette dug her headphones out of her bag. I chewed on my right pinkie nail. "Did you take your vitamin?"

"Uh-huh," Frankie said even quieter, taking the headphones and putting them on. She closed her eyes and didn't say anything else.

Colette turned and gave me a thumbs-up. Carefully, I crept down from the loft, steps creaking behind me as Colette followed. I held tight to the right handrail nailed to the stacked log wall but had nothing to grip on the left: no handrail or wall, either. If I lost my balance and tipped left, I'd fall into the living room.

Apparently, when my great-grandfather built this cabin with his brother way back in the olden days, safety wasn't a big concern. My mom likes to say, "It's hardly up to code," whatever that means. All I know is that I was putting my life in my hands every time I took those stairs.

Thankfully, we made it to the bottom. Colette and I tiptoed across the main common space, knowing one of five adults—Mom, Charles, Aunt Maureen, Uncle Bran, or Grandpa—could appear from the darkened hallway at any moment and tell us to go back to bed. Worse, we could wake up Kennedy's preschooler brother, Kane, and he'd cry, and then we'd really be in for it.

Relief washed over me when my flip-flop hit the gravel driveway outside.

"Here," I said, grabbing the bug spray from the back-porch step and aiming it at my friend. "Otherwise, the horseflies will eat us for a late-night snack."

I shivered, thinking of the angry welts on my legs, then doused Colette in the terrible-smelling spray.

"Use a *lot*," I said, handing her the can.

Coughing through the cloud, we made our way toward the field next to the cabin. We got settled on the boulder big enough for two, both of us hugging our bare knees since it'd gotten cold after the sun went down, staring up at the biggest sky I'd ever seen. It wasn't just above but all around us, a pitch-black background dotted with billions of stars. I felt like I was in a night-sky snow globe.

"I'm really glad my parents let me come with you guys," Colette said. "Pinedale is the coolest."

"I don't know about the *coolest*." I laughed, talking easily with Colette. She was probably the only person I talked that easily with. "Cities that have art galleries and restaurants and stuff are cool. I'd like to go to New York someday. Or Washington, DC. This town only has like four hundred more people than ours."

I meant our home of Long Beach, Washington. In a way, because no big companies had messed with either and they're both pretty far from major cities, Pinedale and Long Beach are similar. But Pinedale's more "Wild West" and surrounded by mountains and lakes, while Long Beach has more of a beach vibe since it's on the Pacific Ocean.

"Frankie told you the population, didn't she?"

"Natch," I said with a laugh. Frankie loves facts.

I looked around at the nothingness and listened to the crickets and breathed the sagebrush and felt calmed by it all. "Yeah, I guess it's pretty great here."

"It's too bad Frankie doesn't think so."

"I know." I swatted away a hovering horsefly, thinking of the epic meltdown Frankie had had the night before, first about having to sleep in the same space as three other people and then about the spider near her bed. Frankie has ADD and is on the autism spectrum, and sometimes things that seem fine to me are massively unfine to her. Then again, even when things were more normal, I worried about dying daily—and Frankie once walked *toward* a tornado—so I guess she's stronger than me in a lot of ways.

"That internet quiz said I definitely have anxiety."

"You needed an internet quiz to tell you that?" Colette said, nudging me with her shoulder. I shrugged. "I don't get why you don't just ask your mom to get you a therapist. I mean, she sends Frankie to one."

"That's why," I said. "Therapists are expensive. She can't afford to send both of us."

"She said that?"

"No, but she would."

I wasn't really sure what she'd say. The truth was that I felt like, if I was really so bad off, my mom would've worried about me in the same way she'd worried about my sister. She would've forced me to go to a therapist already. Instead, she usually just told me to stop biting my nails or worrying so much if I ever brought anything up. She didn't really understand what was going on in my head, and I didn't really want to tell her, because my sister was . . . a lot.

"Anyway, keep going," I said.

Before Frankie had gotten mad, Colette had been telling a ghost story about Crybaby Bridge, some bridge on the East Coast that was rumored to be where a monster threw crying babies who were annoying him over the railing.

Colette did an excited shoulder dance.

"Okay, so! Tons of people commented on the person's post and said that if you go, you can sometimes, very faintly, hear the babies crying!"

"Ohmygod," I said, shaking my head. "That's so terrifying."

"I know, but guess what!"

"What?"

"It's actually goats!"

"Crying ghosts? That's worse."

"No, *goats*," Colette said.

"The monster throws goats?" I asked.

"Ohmygod, Tess." Colette threw her head back and laughed really hard. "No, the cries aren't babies, they're goats! I guess goats sound like crying babies. So, people were getting all freaked out, but it was just goats roaming around, eating grass under the bridge."

"No way!" I said, laughing, too. "I love goats."

"Me too," she said. "Once, at a petting zoo, a goat ate a hole in my T-shirt."

"I've seen them mow an entire field," I said. "They need to mow this!" I waved my hand around in front of us, hitting another horsefly in the dark. They were lurking outside the perimeter of our repellent, waiting to chomp.

Colette shifted on the rock, leaning to one side and then the other to pull her shorts down. "Okay, your turn!"

"Okay," I said, taking a breath, ready to share the story I'd been writing in my mind for weeks. In a low, quiet voice, I said, "Once there was young man named William who fell madly in love with the butcher's daughter, Lilah."

"Did you say the *butcher's* daughter?" Colette said, scooting closer. "That's never good." She gasped. "Look! A falling star!"

"Where?" I asked, searching the sky until I saw the diagonal two-inch streak, brighter on the low end and fading at the top, then disappearing altogether.

"Make a wish."

We both closed our eyes and made wishes but didn't tell each other what they were because then they wouldn't come true.

Colette said, "Keep going."

"Okay, so William and Lilah went out on many romantic dates—"

"What did they do?" Colette interrupted.

I tilted my head to the side and looked at her with an annoyed expression.

"What? I like romantic details."

I laughed, then said, "They went on picnics and to the movies and walks on the beach and stuff, I don't know. Anyway, Lilah fell madly in love with William, too. They talked about going to Paris someday because that was Lilah's dream, to go to chef school in Paris. So, William proposed, and Lilah accepted, and they got married six months later."

"Way to rush into it."

"Shhh," I said, laughing again, feeling her own laughter in my rib cage. We were so squished together we were like one being. "They took over the butcher shop from Lilah's dad and had a great life. For William's birthday one year, Lilah knitted him a beautiful red scarf to keep him warm all the t—"

"Ew, red is ugly," Colette interrupted. "He needs a yellow scarf. Yellow is way happier."

"No men wear yellow scarves."

"I know, he'll be unique!"

"What shade of yellow?" I asked, my art brain taking over.

"I don't know . . . bright?" Colette asked back, laughing.

I sighed. "Fine, she knitted him a bright yellow scarf. He loved it so much he wore it everywhere. But one day, he came home without it, and he told Lilah that he didn't remember where he'd left it. A few weeks later, a beautiful woman rang the doorbell. She was like modelworthy."

"I think I know where this is going. Pumpkin Eater City."

"Totally. So, she says, 'Your husband left this at my house.' Lilah didn't ask any questions; she just slammed the door on the woman and went to confront William, who was working at the butcher shop. She was convinced he was cheating on her!"

"Billy's in trouble."

"His name's William."

"He goes by Billy to his friends."

"He totally doesn't," I said. "And this is my story. Shush your face."

Colette clamped her palm over her mouth, smiling at me with her sparkling eyes. "Go on," she said in a muffled voice.

"No one knows what happened with *William* and Lilah," I said, "but after that day, Lilah was never to be seen again. And William turned really weird, like he'd just walk around and stare at people blankly, all spaced-out and stuff. He'd barely talk to customers and his skin looked bad and he was just . . . strange."

"He was heartbroken," Colette mumbled behind her hand.

"But he still wore his yellow scarf everywhere, even in the summer when it was really hot like it was earlier. The scarf got all smelly and dingy, and people would try to get him to take it off because—gross—and he'd scream at them to get away from him. They all assumed he wore it as a reminder of the long-lost love of his life."

Colette shivered next to me.

"Decades later, William died."

"Of what?"

"I don't know, natural causes. So anyway, Lilah and the beautiful woman who'd brought back the scarf that day were both at his funeral. Lilah had returned to the town for the first time in forever to get closure or whatever. She was mad that the woman was there, too, and that she was still beautiful even though she was older.

"Even in the casket, William had on the gross old scarf with his suit. He'd put in his will that he wanted to be buried in it. After the funeral, the women ended up being the last people in the church. They stood next to William's casket. Lilah said, 'After all these years, I need to know why. Why did he have an affair with you? I thought he loved me! I thought we were so happy!' The other woman gasped and said, 'Oh my goodness! That's what you think? That's not what happened at all! Your tenth anniversary was coming up. William was going to surprise you with a trip to Paris. I'm a language teacher; I was teaching him French!'"

"No way!" Colette said, moving her hand to grip my sweatshirt. "This is insane!"

I giggled, happy that she was into it.

"Then what?" she asked excitedly.

"Then the beautiful woman left Lilah alone in the church with William. Lilah cried over William's body and said she was sorry. Then she left. Since everyone was gone, the priest came back in. He'd been outside giving them space. It was a cold winter day, and he'd seen a homeless person shivering on the steps. He looked at William's body and considered whether he should give the homeless person William's scarf. The priest figured that the casket would be closed before William would be buried, so the family wouldn't know. William was gone, so *he* wouldn't know. And the homeless person wouldn't be so cold, and that was good. The priest decided to take the scarf."

"Ew, don't touch dead William and his dirty scarf!" Colette said quietly. She was gripping my arm so tightly, my hand was starting to fall asleep.

"Well, I think he regretted it, because when the priest removed William's scarf, he realized why William had worn it all those years."

"Why?" Colette asked in a small voice, her eyes huge in the darkness.

"Without the scarf holding it on, William's head fell off."

"GIRLS!" someone snapped harshly.

Colette and I jumped. I don't know who screamed first, but I know I stopped last. Dogs started barking somewhere, and as if that wasn't enough, I heard Kennedy's brother, Kane, start to cry from inside the cabin.

My mom stood under the back porch light with her hands on her hips. "It's after midnight!" she scolded. "Come inside right now!"

Getting down from the rock in a hurry was like rubbing a cheese grater on the back of my bare legs.

"Sorry, Mom," I said as I passed her, my thighs stinging.

"Sorry, Ms. Harper," Colette said when she went by.

"You two are trouble," my mom said in a way that told me we weren't actually *in* trouble. "I know you were just having fun, but it's late, and I really need you to keep it down, okay?"

"Okay," we said in unison.

When we made it back to the loft without dying on the treacherous stairs, Kennedy had flipped over again, but she was still snoring away, and Frankie was asleep, too, still wearing Colette's headphones.

Tucked back in the musty queen-size bed, us now smelling like bug spray and outdoors, I yawned, and Colette did, too.

"So, Lilah chopped off his head?" she whispered.

"Uh-huh," I said, pulling the covers up to my chin.

"And he was a zombie all that time?"

I nodded, making the pillow rustle.

"But then he died again?"

"His zombie body ran out of gas." I laughed quietly, knowing that hadn't really made sense.

"That was a good one," Colette whispered sleepily.

"Yeah, it was okay?" I closed my eyes.

"Nine out of ten."

"Not ten?"

"You're such a perfectionist." *Yawn.*

"I just want to know how I can do better next time," I whispered, yawning, too.

Colette didn't answer for a few seconds. I thought she'd fallen asleep, or maybe I had. Then she whispered groggily, "If you tell the story again, call him Billy."

chapter 1

ALMOST ONE YEAR later, I returned to the cabin in Wyoming. It looked and smelled exactly the same, but everything was different.

Colette had been dead for two and a half months.

"Keep it moving," Kennedy said in her Boston accent, so it sounded like *mah-ving* to me. She bumped my shoulder with her duffel bag, trying to get around me in the cramped cabin entryway. "God, cousin, you're like a rock in a river." *Rivah.*

"Sorry," I murmured, my vocal cords hardly working, taking a step toward the bench that had dirty hiking boots lined up under it, but not setting down my own bag. I'd been pretty much silent during the two-hour solo plane ride from Washington to Salt Lake City and the four-hour rental car ride with my relatives from Salt Lake City to Pinedale.

Frankie had refused to come back, so that meant my mom and her boyfriend, Charles, stayed home, too. I'd been given a choice: go alone—with my Boston relatives, of course—or spend the summer at home.

Here, I'd go to art camp with strangers and try not to annoy my cousin.

There, I'd see the world moving on without Colette firsthand.

That hadn't really been a choice to me.

"I'll carry your bag up, Tess," Uncle Bran said, appearing behind me. "I know you don't like the stairs."

I was very aware of the weight being lifted off my right shoulder as Bran took the bag. I felt like it'd been keeping me from floating away. I sort of wanted it back.

"Thanks," I said weakly. He was already halfway up.

Aunt Maureen tiptoed through the door with five-year-old Kane sleeping in her arms. She lovingly smiled at me before walking down the hallway to put Kane in bed.

"Tess?"

Now Aunt Maureen was standing by the old compact fridge, without Kane, looking at me expectantly. I guess I'd zoned out; who knows for how long.

"Sorry, what?" I asked.

"I asked if you wanted something to drink."

She and Uncle Bran didn't have Boston accents, since they weren't raised there; only their kids did. It was kind of weird.

Aunt Maureen waited patiently for me to answer. I thought about how she was a slightly younger, more put-together version of my mom. Her short-sleeved blue button-down shirt and tan shorts somehow weren't even wrinkled from traveling all day. But my mom had waved me goodbye this morning in dirty sweats and a messy bun.

"I'll get some water," I said.

"I'll get it for you," Aunt Maureen said, motioning me over. "Take a seat."

The round table could fit four people comfortably or six if you didn't mind squishing in. I sat down on one of the outdated chairs. The plastic tablecloth felt sticky even though it was clean. I reached for a faded wooden lemon from the bowl in the center.

Last time I was here, Colette sat across from me. She tried to juggle these lemons. I wonder if she was the last person to touch this.

Aunt Maureen set down my water.

"Are you doing okay?"

Don't ask me that, I thought. *It makes it worse.*

I nodded because talking would make me cry. I felt like crying anyway. I picked up the glass and tried to wash away the lump in my throat.

Uncle Bran and Kennedy thunked down the stairs, across the room, and out the back door.

"Why doesn't she have to help unload the car?" Kennedy asked her dad. I heard her through the screen door.

"She's been through hell," Uncle Bran said. "I think you can manage some kindness for—"

Aunt Maureen shut the inside door.

"Want to go lie down until dinner?"

I didn't want to do anything. "Sure."

I stood up, and Aunt Maureen pulled me into a tight hug.

"Oh, Tessy Bear, you've had a hard time of it, but things will get better. Day by day, it'll get better."

So many adults had said to me: *It'll get better.*

No, it won't, I thought.

Aunt Maureen released me, and I went upstairs, not feeling as terrified of the stairs this time. I walked up the center and barely held on, numb.

In the bunk-room doorway, I looked from right to left at the full-size bed Kennedy had claimed, the two sets of bunk beds on the far wall, and the queen bed to my left. Maybe I should have picked a different place to sleep, but I didn't. I kicked off my shoes, crawled onto the queen bed and under the covers, and snuggled into my spot near the wall, leaving space for someone who wasn't here anymore.

I closed my eyes, thinking of the kids at school. Colette's family. My family.

How did you just keep going?

How did you joke around, signing each other's yearbooks, at the end of a seventh-grade year that Colette didn't finish?

How did you sell the house where she lived?

How do you laugh now when I feel like laughter is a foreign language?

How do you get out of bed without making deals with yourself?

How is Earth even still turning?

"You have an owie."

Startled, I opened my eyes to find my youngest cousin, Kane, next to the bed. I felt out of it, like I'd fallen asleep. His dark blond hair was wild from his own nap. He was looking at my left hand, where the cuticles on three fingers were coated in crusted, dried blood. I'd gotten really good at hiding my hands in pockets or long shirtsleeves after the nail biting had gotten so much worse.

Good job, loser, you're freaking out a little kid.

"That's a bad owie," Kane pointed out again.

"Yeah," I said, tucking my hands under the covers.

"Does it hurt?" he asked with huge, concerned eyes.

He was asking about my hand, but I felt the question

in my heart. "Yeah, it does," I said quietly, which made the tears come. They always came eventually.

Kane reached over and wiped my cheeks dry with his miniature thumbs. "It's okay to cry when you have an owie or just anytime you feel sad."

"Thanks, Kane," I said, so surprised by the gesture that I stopped crying. I wasn't used to being around kids who were younger than me. I didn't have my babysitting certificate yet. Colette and I had been planning to do that together at the end of the summer.

"Okay and Mommy says you have to come to eat your hamburger now please." Kane stared at me for three seconds, then added, "Okay, Teth, you have to get up now Mommy says please. We are having hamburgers and do you like ketchup?"

"I do," I said, sitting up and throwing off the covers.

I followed Kane to the landing. Before he started down, he took my hand and looked up at me with his big eyes and long eyelashes.

"We're going downstairs now," he said bravely, taking a deep breath, then the first step off the landing. "You don't have to be scared. Just hold on tight and go slow."

"Okay, thanks, Kane," I said, getting choked up again.

"Ketchup is icky," he said as we stepped. "I like plain hamburgers. We can still be friends, though, because everyone has their own 'pinions and that's okay. 'Cept my 'pinion is ketchup is very bad and my 'pinion is your 'pinion is wrong."

"Okay," I said.

"Okay," he said.

Me and my little cousin made it down the steps. And then we ate hamburgers.

chapter 2

KENNEDY SAT SHOTGUN, her hand with a black snake thumb ring and a gold band on the middle finger dangling out the window, the wind making the nonshaved side of her dyed-black hair go wild. She rode with her eyes closed, nodding to the aggressive music she'd connected to the rental mini-van's speaker system.

Her dad hadn't seemed to mind it; Uncle Bran was nodding, too, thankfully with his eyes open so he didn't veer the car off the road.

Kennedy had on a gray top with a low neckline and wide arm holes, so I could see her black bra underneath in the reflection in the side mirror. She'd drawn a tiny black heart high on her right cheekbone with eyeliner, just under her eye, and she had on a bunch of necklaces in different lengths with mismatched charms and stones. She looked like she was going to a concert, not the grocery store.

From my seat behind Kennedy, I had a clear view of the speedometer: we were going more than seventy miles per hour. Probably, we weren't even close enough to the shoulder for this to happen, but I still worried more with every mile marker we whooshed by that my cousin's dangling arm would catch on a post or sign or something and be torn off in an instant.

I was always thinking of the worst that could happen. The seed of panic would get planted, watered, and grow and grow until . . .

Kennedy suddenly turned down the music.

"Are you staring at me, Harper?" *Hah-pah.*

Uncle Bran glanced at me in the rearview mirror and then gave Kennedy a look.

"No," I said. "I'm just . . ." I gestured toward the rolling hills of squat, prickly, ankle-scratching sagebrush.

"Didn't look like it," Kennedy said.

"Hey, leave her alone," Uncle Bran said. "Just listen to your music. We'll be there soon enough."

"I don't know why I have to go shopping anyway," Kennedy said.

"Because you want to help your dad." I saw in the side mirror when Kennedy rolled her eyes. "Besides, it'll go faster if we each take part of the list and split up. I need to log on when we're back at the cabin. Not everyone gets to do nothing this summer like you do."

"Whatever," Kennedy said before cranking the music back up.

I looked down at my phone. Frankie had sent me a slow-mo video of our dog, Pirate, digging for a clam on the beach. It was the kind of thing I'd have loved four months ago, but now it just felt stupid.

How can you just casually make videos?

Why aren't you sadder?

Am I the one who's wrong?

I tore a piece of skin from my left thumb with my teeth—the stinging pain making me stop thinking questions at my sister, who was hundreds of miles away and probably wouldn't have had answers that made sense to me anyway. Sometimes, Frankie was the person who got me most in life. Other times, we lived on different planets.

Kennedy grabbed her phone and stopped the music. "I hate this song," she said, thumbing through the options. "I have to find something else."

"You could let Tess choose the next one," Uncle Bran suggested.

"I could," Kennedy said, but didn't ask what I wanted to listen to.

"We're going to have a talk later," Uncle Bran said.

"Can't wait."

In the absence of music, there wasn't really silence, since driving that fast along country roads with the windows down is noisy. I heard rushing wind, the consistent *thunk, thunk, thunk* of the car tires rolling over seams in the pavement, and the occasional *vroom* of cars passing, going just as fast as we were in the opposite direction, unnerving me every time. The sun was high in the vast blue sky.

Suddenly, for a second, it all went away. The road noise muffled and the day dimmed as we drove under a small overpass. I don't know why, but right then, fairies used my spine as a ladder.

I flipped around fast and watched the overpass get farther and farther away. I'd never seen anything like it before. It wasn't a normal overpass that cars could drive across. There wasn't a road on it, only grass connecting one side of the prairie to the other with a barely visible fence instead of a guardrail to protect people from falling off.

"What's that?" I asked, still looking behind us, even though it was making me dizzy to ride like that.

"It's a wildlife crossing," Uncle Bran said. "Don't you remember that from last year? It's safer for the animals. It's mostly for antelope, but all sorts of animals use it."

"So they just built a little hill over the highway and made a tunnel through it?" I asked. We were so far away now, the crossing's archway looked like a mouse hole.

"Yep, to protect the wildlife," Bran said, nodding.

"So they don't get murdered," Kennedy said. *Mah-dahd.*

There's nothing there, dummy, Mean Me said. *Stop staring like an idiot. Don't make them think you're even weirder than they already do.*

"Cool, huh?" Uncle Bran asked.

"Sure," I said, turning back around, still unsettled by . . .

Absolutely nothing! the mean voice hissed. *Get ahold of yourself!*

Kennedy turned on an even worse song, and the rest of the way, I picked at an angry scab on my ring fingernail, licking away the metallic blood when it bubbled up, then pressing the underside of my T-shirt to the wound so it wouldn't bleed more, aware of the uneasy feeling in my middle.

The speed limit lowered, then lowered again, then the highway became Pine Street, the main street through town. We pulled into a huge paved parking lot in front of the general store. There weren't any designated spaces; Uncle Bran just turned off the car next to another one facing the road. He hit the button to open the sliding door.

Kennedy got out and stretched her arms up over her head, revealing most of her abdomen in the process. Two passing teen boys noticed.

"Hey, angel," the taller one said. Tufts of his shaggy blond hair flitted out beneath a camouflage trucker hat. He had on dark swimming trunks and a blue tank top that showed off his farmer's tan.

"Hey," Kennedy said, tilting her chin down and looking at them with her intense, dark-lined eyes. "What's there to do around here?"

"Shopping." Uncle Bran stepped around the side of the car and pointed toward the store. "That's what there is to do around here. Move along, boys."

Kennedy rolled her eyes, then waved to the boys, and they waved back. I don't think they'd even noticed me standing there—me with my plain, straight, dark bister-colored hair, pale skin, and skinny body next to Kennedy with her shocking hair, jewelry, makeup, curves, travel mug of black coffee, and attitude. I felt like she was much more than just a year and a half older than me.

Inside the general store, each of us got a shopping cart and set out with our portion of the grocery list. Like every time I came here, I walked the aisles in slightly horrified fascination. There were the moose, deer, and antelope heads on the walls. Guns and ammunition to the left. Fishing poles and live worms to the right. Need a tent? It's over there. Looking for the perfect fleece blanket? Check aisle three, right next to the paper towels. Saddles. Horse feed. Bear traps. Cozy pajamas. Art from the Wind River Indian Reservation next to framed lyrics of a Grateful Dead song signed by a guy named John Perry Barlow.

And of course, groceries.

I easily gathered up the stuff for taco night, then found

Uncle Bran squinting at the ingredient lists on two jars of what looked like identical pasta sauce.

"I'm done," I said, before remembering my language arts teacher asking if I was a potato. "I mean, I'm finished."

"Great, do you want to help me find a few more things or wait in the car?"

Hmm . . . tomato sauce or alone time? "I'll wait in the car."

"I thought you might say that," he said, smiling. He put one of the jars in his cart and the other back on the shelf, then fished the car keys out of his pocket and handed them to me. "Want me to bring you some fried gizzards?"

"What's a gizzard?" I asked.

"You used to love them when you were a kid."

I looked at him skeptically. "What is it?"

"Chicken," he said, smirking.

"What *part* of a chicken?" I asked out of curiosity, not because I was actually considering eating whatever he was offering. I was about ten minutes from becoming a vegetarian after walking by the in-store butcher shop.

"The stomach part?" He laughed in his way, his shoulders jumping up and down, no sound coming out.

"No, thank you." I felt a smile somewhere deep in me, but it didn't make it to my lips.

Back outside, I found the minivan and got in, leaving the slider open so I didn't get cooked. My weather app said it was eighty degrees, but it felt hotter than what eighty felt like in Long Beach, maybe because it was a lot drier here and closer to the sun. I wondered how fast the stripe of sunlight across my right knee would take to sunburn as I looked around the parking lot, unsettled.

Everything about being here again without Colette felt . . . wrong.

There was a park across the street from the general store, with benches under some fluffy green trees in front of a pond. It looked a lot better than sitting in a hot car, and I was antsy—I needed to move. I texted Uncle Bran that I was going over, and he replied that he'd text when they were checking out.

I crossed at the light and walked into the park, sitting tentatively on the edge of one of the benches. I realized that the park was bigger than I'd thought: the pond and path stretched pretty far away from the street into a more wooded area. A few people were walking dogs or jogging on the path, disappearing into the trees, then reemerging out the other side.

There was a group of kids about my age messing around on scooters, trying to flip them over their heads and stuff. One of the kids noticed me, so I got up and started walking on the path, moving away from them.

I didn't want to be noticed.

I felt like I was being watched until the path curved into the cluster of trees. I couldn't see the road or the general store anymore—and people over there couldn't see me. As I checked my phone to make sure I hadn't missed a text from Uncle Bran, a breeze tickled the hairs on my arms and made me shiver. Maybe the walk would have been nice if my brain had shut up.

What if I get attacked by a bear and no one helps me?

What if I get stung by a bee and that's when I realize I'm allergic to them?

What if I die and no one has any idea where I am? Just like no one knew where Colette was after she fell into a ravine.

A jogger startled me, appearing from around the bend. I kept my head down as he ran by, picturing him suddenly turning around and strangling me.

You really are mental, said the mean voice in my head.

I picked up the pace, my legs burning and my right shoe ripping open a blister as I made my way through the forested area. I realized I'd have to walk right by the kids on the scooters eventually unless they'd moved on.

I checked my phone for missed texts again.

My heart hammered in my chest.

Nothing is even happening, said the mean girl in my head. *Why can't you just be normal? Most kids don't worry about every-thing like you do. Why are you so weird?*

As I finally broke through the cluster of trees, relief washed over me: I'd made it full circle. I could see the cars driving on Pine Street in the distance, the general store just beyond. I felt like I'd survived a haunted house instead of a walk in a nice park in broad daylight.

The kids with the scooters weren't there anymore.

I slowed down, feeling stupid, hating on myself.

That runner must have thought you were a freak.

Everyone thinks you're a freak.

Because YOU ARE!

My phone buzzed; I checked the message.

UNCLE BRAN

Paying for your fried gizzards now . . .
see you at the car!

I stopped walking to send vomit and thumbs-up emojis, then put the phone back in my pocket. That was when I realized there was someone sitting on a bench about ten feet from me.

The man was old, with wispy white hair, sunken cheeks, tan pants, dark circles under his eyes, and shoes with thick soles. His frail hands clutched the plaid blanket that was wrapped around his shoulders . . . in eighty-degree weather. I smiled at him, because I'd been taught to be polite to old people, but he just stared back with intense, cloudy gray eyes.

It made me nervous, but I know sometimes old people aren't all there. I thought maybe he needed some space, or maybe he was blind and deaf and didn't even know I was nearby. But when I took a step to walk away, he tapped his foot. I took another step, and he did it again. Every time I stepped, the man tapped.

Step . . . tap.

Step . . . tap.

Step . . . tap.

I shivered, wishing he'd stop. Wanting to tell him to but feeling like I had to be polite. He was old, after all.

Maybe it's his way of playing a game, I thought, trying to chill out.

I tried smiling at him again, but he just stared back, even more intensely. He didn't seem blind or deaf—or friendly, either. Spooked, I walked faster. The man tapped faster.

Step . . . tap.

Step-tap.

Steptap.

Steptap.

Steptap.

Soon I couldn't hear the tapping anymore because I was running and almost at the park's exit, my heartbeat pounding in my ears and muffling everything else. Thankfully, the light was in my favor, so I crossed without having to wait, rushing back to the parking lot.

"How was the park?" Uncle Bran asked when I reached the minivan.

"Fine," I said, out of breath.

Uncle Bran put the groceries in the trunk, and we all got in.

"Everything okay?" he asked. Kennedy eyed me in the mirror.

"Fine," I repeated.

"Okay, then," Uncle Bran said, putting the minivan in reverse and backing out of the not-space. "Well, I skipped the gizzards, but I did get an apple pie."

"Thanks," I said weakly, eyes on the park entrance. No one was there.

Uncle Bran waited for the cars to pass before turning onto Pine. I kept my eyes on what I could see of the park, my heartbeat refusing to slow down, like it knew something was going to happen and wanted to be ready. And then it did: just before we turned the corner, the old man walked into view. He waited at the light, looking across, right at us. Right at me? No, because he couldn't see me behind Kennedy, but was he looking *for* me?

As he waited, the man's blanket dropped from his shoulders just for a second before he rewrapped himself. Uncle Bran turned onto Pine toward the cabin, and the man faded into the distance, while I shivered in the too-hot back seat, the fairies scrambling up my spine again. I couldn't believe what I'd just seen.

In eighty-degree weather, the old man had been wearing a scarf.

But not just any scarf.

It was a yellow one.

Like William's.

chapter 3

"WHY ARE YOU calling so early?"

I had the phone on speaker; tears filled my eyes at the sound of my fraternal twin sister's scratchy voice. It wasn't just that it was morning: her voice always sounded like that. It was mesmerizing, even if she was saying . . .

"Seriously! What's the emergency? Because that's the only reason you should call me before ten."

"Hey, Frankie," I said, hugging my bare knees with my left hand, holding the phone with my right. "Sorry I woke you up."

"You didn't," she said. "You interrupted my daydream."

"Oh. Sorry." I shifted to get more comfortable. Not wanting to wake Kennedy, I'd crept outside to sit on the boulder that was big enough for two. Of course, it was just me on it this morning. I wasn't in the middle, though. I'd left space for Colette.

Stupid. She's gone!

"So, what's up?" Frankie said before a long, drawn-out yawn, all casual, like I was in my room right next to hers at the inn where we lived. Like I wasn't several states away. Like she didn't miss me at all.

"Nothing, I just wanted to say hi to you," I said, deflated. "Mom told me to check in with you guys, and I hadn't had a chance ye—"

"Uh-huh," Frankie interrupted. "Got it."

I heard covers rustling like she was rolling over. I pictured her comforter halfway off her bed; her wavy dark brown hair with a nest in the back; her chocolate eyes with dark circles under them; the floor of her room littered with books, clothes, and papers . . . like usual. The thought made me feel like my insides were melted caramel.

Another call came in: a video call . . . from Frankie.

Sighing, I answered it.

"Hi," I said, smoothing my hair self-consciously since I could see myself now.

A pang of homesickness hit me when Frankie filled the screen. She looked exactly as I'd pictured her. She had on a gray tank top with a blue strap showing underneath, and her bangs were so long, hitting the top of her cheekbones.

Behind her, the window was open, making the sheer white curtain billow in with the breeze.

"I miss home," I said, imagining the smell of the ocean through the screen.

"Yeah," Frankie said. "So, what's up?" she repeated. Frankie wasn't a small-talk kind of person.

"Nothing, I just . . ." *I called because I wish you'd called me. I wish you'd ask me if I'm okay. I know you won't.* "How are you doing?"

"Fine." She stared at herself.

"I mean about Colette," I clarified. It'd been two and a half months since she'd died. The time that'd gone by felt like forever and five minutes at the same time.

"I know, I'm fine."

"You're . . . *fine*?" She sounded like Colette had meant nothing to her, which I knew wasn't true. Still, it was frustrating how, on the outside, Frankie seemed completely okay. "I don't understand why you're not sadder," I admitted without thinking. Often, I filtered what I said to my sister, fearing she'd get upset. Maybe it was the distance that made me feel braver, but today I didn't hold back. "I don't get why I'm the only one who seems to be breaking down."

"You seem fine to me," Frankie said plainly, surprising me by not yelling about what I'd said. "Gabe says everyone grieves in their own way." Gabe was Frankie's therapist. "You cry; I don't. It's not like I don't miss her."

"Okay," I said. "It's just . . ."

Other people might have asked, "Just what?" Frankie didn't.

The conversation wasn't making me feel better, so I decided to switch topics. "Hey, did Colette ever tell you the ghost story about William and Lilah?"

"I hate ghost stories. Why would she tell me one?" Frankie kept her eyebrows natural instead of plucking them, so when she pulled them together, like right now, it was dramatic.

"Nothing, I thought—" A horsefly landed on my knee with its gigantic coal-colored body; I quickly flicked it away before it took a bite. "I told the story to Colette when we were here last summer, and yesterday in a park, I saw someone who reminded me of William."

"Who's William?"

"The guy in the ghost story."

"Is he real?"

"No, Frankie, I made him up," I said, rolling my eyes. "But then I saw someone who looked like how I pictured the guy."

"Cool." My sister was making faces at herself in the camera. She currently had her mouth open as wide as it would go. I could see she needed to floss more.

"It was scary, actually."

"You think everything is scary," Frankie said, hurting

my feelings. "It's weird you like haunted houses and scary books so much when they freak you out."

I don't as much now.

"It was our thing, mine and Colette's," I said.

"Duh." She clenched her jaw and started snarling at the camera like a wolf. Through her teeth, she asked, "What did the guy in the park do?"

"He looked at me in a creepy way and followed me out," I said confidently, even though it was possible he hadn't actually followed me but just left on his own.

"Cool."

Frankie said *cool* a lot. It was almost always a sign she was only half listening. She started alternating exaggerated "ooh" and "aah" faces.

"And he tapped his foot every time I took a step when I went by him. It was so weird. I mean, who does that?"

"Like Colette's soundtrack game," Frankie interrupted.

"What game?" I asked, hugging myself tighter, shivering for no reason. I looked around the prairie; no one was nearby.

"It was really stupid," Frankie said flatly. "It was one of those recess games . . . like jail and jumper."

"I remember those," I said, a creepy feeling spreading through my body. "What was the soundtrack game?" I waited as Frankie contorted her face a few more times. "Frankie! Will you look at me and answer?"

"I can do two things at once," she replied, now admiring her extreme close-up. "One kid walked or ran or hopped around as quietly as they could and someone else tried to make the sounds that matched their movements. The third person was the judge." She looked at the lens for maybe the first time. "See? Stupid. That's why you don't remember it."

"I sort of do," I said, curling deeper into a ball. "But . . . why would the man . . ." It didn't make sense.

Frankie turned the phone so she was upside down. In a monotone voice, she said, "Maybe he's a ghost messenger and Colette's trying to communicate with you."

"Ohmygod, Frankie!" I said, holding the phone out from my face, scared and annoyed at the same time. "That's such a terrible thing to say!"

"No, it isn't." She turned the phone again, then set it down so all I could see was the white ceiling. Frankie had put a sticky note up there; I couldn't read what it said. "I'm just kidding."

"It's *not* funny."

"Ghost messengers aren't real. *Ghosts* aren't even real," she said. "I watched a documentary on what happens after we die. Spoiler alert: it's nothing. We just disappear."

The ceiling in Frankie's room didn't notice I suddenly had tears streaming down my face. Neither did my sister, whose volume had gotten faint like she was across the room doing something else. These days, I felt like a balloon with tears instead of helium inside, and the tiniest pinprick would make them leak out.

"Aunt Maureen has breakfast ready," I said, trying to make my voice sound sturdy. "I'd better go. Will you tell Mom I'll call her and Charles later?"

"Uh-huh, yeah," Frankie said. I knew she'd probably forget. "Bye."

She thudded across her bedroom, and I saw her thumb come in close. The call disconnected.

Half an hour later, when breakfast really was ready, my phone buzzed with a new text. The phone stuck to the tablecloth when I picked it up.

FRANKIE

Sorry

I sent back a question mark, then:

TESS

For what?

For making you cry.

I didn't think you noticed

I notice everything

41

> Thanks. I accept

Accept what?

> Your apology

That's such a weird thing to say
I accept
So frmal
*formal

> Sorry

It always came back to that. To me being the one to apologize.

Her read receipt told me that she saw my response, but she didn't write back. I left things there, too, not wanting to talk in circles. And her apology had helped.

That doesn't mean I stopped thinking about the seed Frankie had planted in my brain, about Colette trying to contact me. The mean voice shouted in my head that it was a ridiculous thing to consider, but looking back, I see that's when it started. I wonder if things would have gone differently if I'd never called my sister that morning.

Or maybe it all would have happened no matter what.

chapter 4

AFTER A RESTLESS night in and out of dreams I couldn't remember in the morning, it was time to start art camp.

The whole ride there in the minivan, I stared out the window, my shoulders so tight they were creeping up to my earlobes. When we went under the animal crossing, even though the windows were closed this time, I got the same spine-tingling feeling when the world went dimmer for a brief second.

I quickly turned around to look back at it; still there was nothing.

You're scared of an overpass! Mean Me sneered. *There is seriously something wrong with you.*

When the speed limit slowed and we'd made it to town, I checked every corner, expecting the yellow-scarf-wearing man to be wandering the streets, looking for me. As much as I knew that was a silly thing to think, I thought it anyway.

I bit down hard on my finger, until I realized Kane was watching me with concern.

"Sorry," I said, gripping the armrest.

"No more owies, Teth," Kane said. Aunt Maureen glanced at me in the rearview mirror but didn't say anything as she took a right turn off of Pine.

Camp took place at the local library. I'd insisted that Aunt Maureen drop me off outside, but when we pulled up in front of the barn-red-and-wood modern-rustic building, inside I screamed, *COME WITH ME!*

On top of that, I felt sick about having to meet new people.

I'd met my best friend in kindergarten and had only made one new friend in middle school, this girl named Mia. But Colette had brought Mia into our friend group—I hadn't done anything.

Like Kane could hear my thoughts, he reached across the space between his booster seat and my regular one to put his kind-of-sticky but super-soft hand on mine, careful to touch the back of my hands and not my bloody fingers.

"Don't worry, Teth, it's okay. Just smile and be nice, and everyone will like you and want to make a playdate. Just don't tell them you like ketchup."

"Thanks, Kane," I said.

"Bring me a picture?" he asked, blinking at me with cartoon eyes. "I like green but not purple so no purple okay thank you please, Teth."

"I don't know if we're going to do that kind of art today," I said.

Blink blink. "Okay, but will you bring me a picture?" Kane asked. "One with green?"

"But—"

"I want a picture please okay, Teth, thank you."

I wondered if he was going to grow up to be a professional negotiator. Aunt Maureen had turned around in her seat and was smiling like she thought the whole thing was adorable.

"Okay, fine," I said, "I'll bring you a picture."

"With green."

"Yes, with green in it." I pushed the button on the sliding door and stepped out. "Thanks for the ride," I said to my aunt.

"We'll be back to get you at three," she said. "You got your sack lunch, right?" I nodded once. "Okay, try to have fun, Tessy Bear. I know it's hard right now, but just give it a shot."

"I will."

"BYE, TETH!!!" Kane shouted at the top of his lungs, even though I was still standing next to the car. He flapped both hands like he was trying to wave and fly away at the same time. "HAVE A GOOD DAY, TETH!!!"

"Bye, Kane," I said, waving and shutting the door. I heard him start to sing "We Will Rock You" by Queen before the slider closed all the way.

The library was nicer than any building we had in Long Beach. I'd heard Aunt Maureen and Uncle Bran talking about how this county was rich because of natural gas, so it had things like a sparkling new library and middle school, beautiful parks, and an aquatic center, even though some of the stores on Pine still had wood-plank sidewalks out front.

I took a big gulp of air and went inside, looking up at the high, slanting ceiling with massive beams, and smelling both new construction and old books at the same time. I followed signs through the stacks to the meeting room where the art camp would be held.

"Welcome!" said the only person in the room when she saw me hovering. The woman had long, wavy blond hair and wore a maxi dress with an open-front cardigan and flat sandals. "I'm Karly Blythe. I'll be your art teacher for the next five weeks. What's your name?"

"Tess Harper," I said numbly.

"*Ah*, it's so nice to meet you, Tess," she said in a knowing way, and I wondered if my mom or aunt had told her about me in advance.

"You too, Ms. Blythe."

"Oh my goodness, call me Karly!" She tossed her hair over her shoulder. "I'm too young to be Ms. Anything." She laughed at her own joke, then cleared her throat. "Since you're the first to arrive, you get first pick of the work spaces." She waved a hand toward the rows of tables. "Sit anywhere you like!"

Her voice echoed; the room was huge. Karly went back to whatever she'd been doing while I looked around.

The walls were stacked logs—or made to look like them. The one without the row of windows had different styles of art framed in black, all hung at my eye level. The floor had a massive circular labyrinth pattern etched into it, like the people who built the library had wanted to summon aliens from outer space. Heavy beams supported the ceiling in an alternating pattern of raw wood and sturdy black metal. It was pretty and well-lit and a nice place to create art.

For other people, that is. I hadn't made anything since . . . before.

Biting a piece of skin from the inside of my lip, I chose a table in the second row near the center and sat down. Feeling weird about being the first one there, I decided to find something to do. I didn't have a book, and I'd turned off my social media because I hadn't wanted to watch everyone back at home living life without Colette. So, I opened Viewer, but instead of checking which videos were trending, I went to my own account.

Well, *our* account.

"Let's make up a password so no one else can get in," Colette had said to me and Frankie when we'd created the Viewer account back in third grade. We'd been in Colette's pink-everything bedroom, sitting cross-legged around the laptop on her floor. We made the account as a place to keep videos of us playing our made-up dare-or-scare game. "Not even our parents will be able to see it."

"I asked Mommy's permission to make the account," I admitted.

"That's dumb," Frankie said. "Viewer's for kids. You don't need permission."

"Let's just make a password, okay?" Colette said, looking at me. "You can give it to your mom if you want."

"No," Frankie said. "She can't."

"Or you can think of it like a lock on a diary?" Colette suggested.

That had made sense to my third-grader brain, and I'd agreed. Years later, police would make me and Frankie remove the password so they could look through the dare-or-scare videos to make sure they hadn't missed anything before they called Colette's death "accidental" and closed the case. After that, Frankie or I could've added a new password, but it hadn't seemed like there was a point. Who cared anymore?

Colette had died re-creating our game.

I silenced my phone and picked an old video at random. In it, Frankie and Colette were struggling to pull themselves up on a chin-up bar at the park. Both of their faces were rounder, and they had crooked or missing teeth and wore cheesy inspirational T-shirts. Plus, they were laughing hysterically.

Their laughter made me feel like crying, so I closed Viewer.

A lot of other kids had arrived anyway.

But just before camp started, I sent a text.

TESS

I miss you so much it feels like I have the flu.

I hit send and felt the phone vibrate as I set it on the desk facedown. I didn't want to see the "number unavailable" message bounce back, like usual. Colette's parents had disconnected her phone service two weeks after her death, but I hadn't deleted her contact info from my phone. And I hadn't stopped texting her either.

I didn't think I ever would.

"Now that we're all settled, I'd like to welcome you to art camp!" Karly said enthusiastically—maybe too much, or maybe I was just bothered by everyone right then. "I'm excited to hang out with you this summer."

I felt like I was underwater, so it was a miracle I heard anything Karly said in those first few minutes of camp. I did miss some things, but I know she talked about growing up in the area and teaching art at the high school. Maybe she said something about having a dog? Or a cat? Or a baby?

I tried hard to listen when she told us about what we were going to learn at camp.

"Over the next five weeks, you'll work in several different visual arts mediums, from painting to sculpture to mixed media to collage. Of course, since this is summer camp, we'll also take some breaks for fun excursions, too, like a trip to the aquatic center and walks to give us inspiration for our work!"

As she went on, I stuck my finger in my mouth and bit down. I was not a specialist in *every* kind of art. In fact, I could draw, and that was it. I worried that I'd mistakenly gotten accepted to camp and was expected to be good at *all* art types.

You don't belong here, Mean Me said. *You're going to humiliate yourself.*

I refocused on Karly, who looked as excited as a host of a preschool TV show. She raised her eyebrows and opened her eyes wide as she said, "We'll try things like manga, collage, splatter art, and photography! You'll try new styles, but you'll each have one big project to complete in your own preferred medium. It's going to be so much fun! And remember, this is a creative, supportive environment." She looked at me. "Art is a great way to express any feelings you may be working through in your life right now. And my hope is that you'll strengthen friendships or make new ones."

I didn't want any new friends. I wanted Colette.

And besides, everyone here probably already knew each other.

"With that in mind," Karly went on, "we're going to spend today doing some icebreaker exercises. Many of you may have had classes together during the school year, but it's important that you all feel comfortable with each other, because we will be doing presentations and critiques."

I slumped in my chair. This was getting worse by the second.

"I'm going to group you into four teams of six," Karly said, picking up a piece of paper. "You have thirty minutes to learn as much about your teammates as you can. Then we're going to do an activity to show how much you learned. When I call your name, stand up, and we'll . . ."

I forgot the rest.

———

IN THE BACK of the meeting room near the wall of windows that looked out toward the spiky peaks of what Uncle Bran had told me was the Wind River Mountain Range, I stood with my hands clasped together so tightly several of my fingers were turning white.

"Let's say three things about ourselves, but weird stuff so we can all remember it," said a take-charge girl, clearly a student body president or leader of the debate team or most valuable soccer player. Her hair was cut short and she wore a T-shirt that said ABLE. "I'm Jasmine, but like most of you know that." She rolled her eyes, and a few people laughed. "Here are my three things. First, my brother plays professional football."

A girl to my right sighed heavily, tossing her shiny black hair with dramatic blond streaks over her shoulder, eyes on her phone. "Really?" she asked sarcastically, but it sounded playful, not mean. "As if anyone doesn't know that."

"She might not," Jasmine said, pointing in my direction. "Or him. Who are you guys, anyway?"

"Rude much?" the other girl said.

"Sam, stop interrupting," Jasmine said.

"Stop bragging about your brother," Sam said with a smile.

"Hey, I'm Sam, too!" said a boy with a neat haircut wearing a fitted, short-sleeved button-down shirt and slip-on canvas shoes. "I just moved here from Park City."

"No way!" said curvy, texting Girl Sam. "Then we're new best friends!"

Everyone laughed except me. Nothing felt funny.

"What about you?" Girl Sam said, turning my way. "What's your story?"

"I'm Tess, and I'm from Long Beach." I felt like a mouse.

"California?" Boy Sam asked, stepping toward me, maybe to hear me better, eyes sparkling like he thought California was the best place on the planet.

"No, Washington," I said. He stepped back, looking disappointed.

"I didn't know there was a Long Beach in Washington," Jasmine said, tilting her head at me, confused.

"There is." They were all staring, making my cheeks burn. "It's near the border of Washington and Oregon. It's tiny."

"Pinedale's a speck, too," Jasmine said, shrugging one shoulder like small towns were fine with her. "What brings you here? Did you move like Sam did?"

I shook my head, wishing they'd stop asking questions and that someone would give me water. My mouth felt like I'd eaten glue, my voice was higher than normal, and I couldn't get a deep breath.

"I'm just visiting."

"Where are you staying?" Girl Sam asked.

"At our cabin?" I asked back. She stared at me like she wanted the address. "It's on 191 in the direction of Jackson Hole."

Girl Sam smirked, and a couple other people outright chuckled.

"No one calls it Jackson Hole," a boy said. "If you want to talk like a local, call it Jackson." He smiled with perfectly straight white teeth that stood out against his olive skin. He was about an inch taller than me, with dark, super-curly hair. "I'm Izzy."

He looked at Jasmine and held up a finger. "I love Fire Hot Cheese Crisps." He held up another finger. "My mom set our kitchen on fire last summer." He held up a third. "Firestorm is an underrated character."

"Wrong," another boy said flatly.

"That's not about you, Izzy," Jasmine said. "It's about . . ." She looked around the group for help.

"A comic book character," Girl Sam said, rolling her eyes. "A *DC* one."

"DC sucks," said a tall, dark, and wiry boy standing closer to Jasmine than Izzy.

Boy Sam gasped, eyes wide like the kid had offended him. "Harley Quinn is the reason I get out of bed in the morning."

Girl Sam lost it. "But Aquaman?"

"Every franchise has its faults," Boy Sam admitted sheepishly.

"People, can we like reel it in here?" Jasmine asked. Then, to Izzy, "Say something about you, not a comic book character."

"Fine," Izzy said. "*I* once ate a ghost pepper."

"I'm sensing a theme here," Girl Sam muttered. "Everything's about fire. Are you saying you're hot or something, because you're not all that."

"No, *Samantha*, I'm sharing three things related to hotness so you guys can easily remember them if there's a quiz or something."

"There aren't quizzes at art camp," Jasmine said, looking concerned. "Are there?"

"I'm Jake," said the kid who'd told Izzy he was wrong about Firestorm—loudly. He was looking at me as his black-framed glasses slipped down his nose; he didn't push them back up. His messy hair was greasy, and his cargo shorts and maroon polo looked like he'd worn them yesterday and slept in them last night, too. "I'm neighbors with Izzy, I'm very good at photography, and Jackson Hole is correct." His sleepy eyes fell back to his super-scuffed sneakers. "Oh, and I take German."

The way he talked immediately reminded me of my sister, especially when she was younger. I wondered if Jake was on the autism spectrum.

"Nice," Izzy said to Jake. Then, to me, "We all go to school together. Well, except Sam. But I guess we will, too?"

Boy Sam said, "Looks that way."

I felt like such an outcast.

Why did you come here? Mean Me asked. *What, did you think you were just going to do some art and be over what happened? How stupid are you?*

"Tess?" Izzy asked.

I stared at him blankly. "Huh?" I realized he had nice eyes. They looked like caramel sunbursts in front of a chocolate background.

"We were asking about what you like to do?"

"I don't really . . ." I said, my voice trailing off. "I mean, I draw."

"That's cool," Izzy said quietly, smiling.

"But like what do you do with your friends?" Jasmine asked. It was a regular thing to ask, but they didn't know what had happened. They didn't know what a huge, gaping hole Colette had left in my life.

The tears tried to fill it. Except they were just salt water, and Colette had been a living, breathing, 116-pound human with red hair and bright eyes and confetti freckles and the best hugs and the loudest laugh and the fiercest love.

And tears were just tears.

They couldn't fill anything.

I ran out of the classroom.

chapter 5

"THAT TEACHER MADE me come get you," Girl Sam said from outside the bathroom stall. I heard her pop her gum and double-tap her long fingernails on her phone. "You good?"

"I feel like an idiot," I admitted, staring at my sandals, which were basically too small. My mom hadn't noticed my toes almost hanging over the edges, and I hadn't wanted to point it out before I left. "Who runs out of class like that?"

"I've seen it happen," Girl Sam said casually. "Besides, it's not real school. It's just camp. It's not like you'll get an 'unexcused' or whatever." She waited a few seconds. "Just say your dog died or something, and everyone will be cool."

"My best friend died recently," I replied softly, without thinking.

Good going, oversharer. No one wants to be friends with some-one who just drops their issues on their doorstep like a bag of flaming poop.

"Ohmygod," Girl Sam said. It sounded like she put her hand on the stall door. "That's . . . I'm really sorry I said that. I didn't mean it."

"It's okay," I said. "Just don't . . . I don't really want to talk about it. I don't know why I told you that."

"Maybe you felt like you were at confession?" she said with a nervous laugh, popping her gum again. I didn't get the joke.

"Just don't say anything, okay?"

"No problem," Girl Sam said. "You don't know me, but I have a reputation as a vault." She paused. "Like, there was this really big rumor going around last year, and I knew the truth and didn't tell anyone because I'd been sworn to secrecy." She still sounded nervous. "But like even though you don't know me, if you want to talk about it, I am also a good listener. I'm just saying."

"Thanks, Sam, that's really nice." I stood up and opened the stall door, then smiled at her as best I could. "I'm ready to go back now."

⌒‿⌒

AFTER A MORNING of icebreakers and a drawing project—I made sure to use green pencil for Kane—we ate our sack lunches under the trees surrounding the library, then left for our first "inspirational activity." No one asked me why I'd run out of class, and Girl Sam didn't say anything or even look at me differently, which I appreciated.

As the herd of twenty-four middle schoolers moved toward Pine Street, Karly walked backward like a tour guide, talking nonstop. A librarian followed behind to make sure no stragglers got lost, which was kind of funny, considering everyone knew where they were going except me, and even I could have found my way back to the cabin.

I trailed behind a group of three kids and was sort of next to Jasmine and a boy, but not with them, trying to listen to Karly while also freaking out, checking street corners for the old man.

"Most of you have lived here the majority of your lives," Karly said, "but I want to challenge you to see it with fresh eyes. Tomorrow, we'll be creating collage art inspired by today's journey, so I hope you'll take pictures to remind yourself of what you find interesting."

"Did she say *collage*?" whispered the wiry boy who was now walking hand in hand with Jasmine. I realized that was why he'd been standing close to her inside: they were a thing. He laughed with a snort, ducking down and covering his mouth so he didn't get in trouble. "Like in kindergarten?"

"Shh," Jasmine said, smacking him. "Collage is legit. Ever heard of Man Ray?"

I hadn't, so I felt less unworthy of art camp when the boy said, "Uh, no? I've heard of a manta ray, though." He shook his head at Jasmine. "I can't believe you talked me into this."

"It's better than playing video games all summer long," Jasmine said.

"Says who?"

Jasmine saw me watching them. She hooked a thumb at the boy and said, "My uncultured boyfriend, Axl."

"What's up?" Axl said, lifting his chin.

"What's . . . hi," I said quietly.

Way to be awkward, loser. No wonder you've never had a boyfriend yourself. You're probably going to grow up to be a friendless, boyfriendless cat lady.

I refocused on Karly, who was talking about some historic motel we were about to pass. Apparently, it was once sold as part of a poker game and was used as a birthing center in the old days.

"Because of the harsh winters around here, doctors couldn't get to the ranches, so women would come and stay at this motel to have their babies," Karly said excitedly. "As you can see, it's been lovingly maintained in its original log-cabin style. Beautiful!"

"More like *boring*," Girl Sam said. I hadn't noticed, but she'd walked up beside me. Izzy was on her other side.

"I think it's kind of cool," he said, taking a selfie with the motel behind him. "I've gone by this place a gazillion times and never stopped to look at it."

Girl Sam rolled her eyes at him. "I want to do cartoons, not collages. And it's too hot out here to be walking around staring at stuff we've already seen. How's that *inspiring*?" Her hand shot up in the air. Loudly, she said, "Karly? Can we stop for a drink?"

"In half an hour we'll get a snack and then double back through the park," Karly said. "Let's head down this way and take note of the architecture . . ."

My ears tingled like I was being watched. I looked left, right, in front of, and behind me. I didn't see the old man anywhere.

Girl Sam melted into the group behind us and started animatedly talking to Boy Sam like they'd known each other their whole lives.

Good job being a mute and making her not want to talk to you.

"How many parks are there here?" I asked Izzy, trying not to let my worry seep into my tone, forcing myself to be social.

"Uh . . ." he said, scrunching up his forehead. "Two? Maybe three? There's Veteran's . . . that's where they do the Fourth of July celebration, which you just missed, and then there's Skinner." He tilted his head to the side. "Wait, did you mean national parks?"

"No, like which one is basically . . ." I turned around in circles to see where we were in relation to where I thought the general store was, then pointed. "Basically right over there."

"That's Skinner." He smiled. "My house is close to it."

I hoped that Skinner wasn't the park we were going to walk through, because I was afraid the old man would be there, waiting for me, tapping his feet as I walked by. Trying to tell me something?

The weight of being watched was heavy on my shoulders.

"Earth to Tess," Izzy said, waving his hand in front of my face.

"Sorry, what did you say?" I asked.

"I asked if you were okay," Izzy said, looking at me with a funny expression. "Because no offense, but you seem sorta out of it. And you ran out earlier?"

"I came back," I said quietly.

"I know, but . . ." He let that hang there while he patted his hair, which he'd piled up in a topknot. It was a look that could have been retro in a bad way but somehow worked on him. He had the kind of sturdy features that could support any hairstyle, probably.

"I'm just . . ."

Keeping an eye out for an old man stalker?

Afraid of a deer crossing?

Worried my dead best friend is trying to talk to me?

62

"Whoa," Izzy said, looking horrified. "Doesn't that hurt?"

I hadn't realized I'd been biting the skin around my thumb. I took it out of my mouth, glancing at the raw and bleeding mess before I wiped it on the side of my denim shorts.

"Bad habit," I said, my face getting hot. I must have been tomato red. "Sorry."

"You don't need to say sorry to me," Izzy said. "Maybe to your thumb, though." When I didn't laugh, he said, "Bad joke."

He looked like he wanted to melt into the crowd of kids, too. Instead, he pointed up the street we'd turned onto, which didn't have sidewalks, just like some of the neighborhood streets at home. The familiarity calmed me.

"I flipped over my handlebars right up there when I was ten," Izzy said. "I literally skidded across the pavement on my face."

My eyes wide, I couldn't help but check his face for scars. The only thing I saw was enviably clear skin. I touched the painful mound on my chin I knew would turn into a pimple soon, then put my hand away, thinking of my mom warning me that touching it would only make it worse.

"Were you okay?" I asked.

"It hurt, but yeah," he said, laughing. "Mostly I was embarrassed because I'd been trying to ride no-handed."

"Uh . . . why?" I asked.

"Because Ella McDonald was watching." It was subtle, but he blushed.

I rolled my eyes, thinking boys did strange things to get girls' attention.

"My best friend did that once," I said quietly.

"Tried to impress Ella McDonald?"

I sighed and shook my head. "She hit a pothole and went over the handlebars. But she landed in the grass." I paused, scratching a horsefly bite near my elbow, remembering Colette. "She wasn't riding no-hands, though; she was just terrible at riding bikes."

"She's luckier than I am, then," Izzy said.

No, she's not. You're alive.

"When my family came here last summer, she came with us," I said, following the kids ahead, turning onto Pine.

"Oh, yeah?" Izzy asked, pulling at the front of his T-shirt a few times to let in some air. "Why didn't she come this year? Cooler places to go?"

Tell the truth and sound pathetic.

Tell a story and be a liar.

"Looks like we're stopping," I said instead, pointing at the Mexican restaurant with a porch overhang held up by two logs. It seemed like everything here was made of logs.

"Sweet, that place is killer," Izzy said.

Karly announced that she'd buy us all chips and guaca-mole using the snack money our parents had paid with camp fees, then held open the door to the restaurant, smiling at everyone but saying an especially syrupy "Hi, Tess" as I went by. I took one more look around outside to make sure . . .

What? Stop doing that!

Everything inside the restaurant looked like it had a golden filter on it. The booths were medium wood with intricate carvings in the sides, and the lighter wood tables and walls looked gold in the afternoon light. The smell of fried tortillas and taco meat hit me, making my stomach rumble. I hadn't eaten much of my breakfast or lunch; it was hard to eat with a constant pit of nerves taking up all the room in my stomach.

Everyone was sorting into small groups and filling the booths, but I just stood in the center like the rock in a river my cousin thought I was.

Jasmine and Axl sat with two kids I hadn't met yet.

Jake sat opposite Karly and the librarian, telling kids who walked over to find another table because he needed a side of the booth to himself.

"Izzy!" a girl called, waving at him. I hadn't noticed her until then. She had long blond hair, bright blue eyes, and a tan made even tanner against her short white shorts and white crop top. I thought she looked like the daughter of Captain America.

That's a Colette line, Mean Me pointed out. *Get your own material.*

"We have room!" the girl said to Izzy, poking her friend in the ribs so she'd scoot over.

"Thanks, Jackie," Izzy said with a wave, but he didn't join her. Instead, he scanned the room for Girl Sam and started walking toward the table where she and Boy Sam were sitting. "Come on," he said, looking back at me. "Sit with us."

I settled in next to Girl Sam, across from Izzy. They all started talking about the proper salt-to-grease ratio on chips, and I tried to listen and relax and just be in the moment and maybe even be open to making some new friends. But I couldn't shake the tension; I still felt like I was being watched.

"I'm going to wash my hands," I said.

"It's back there," Girl Sam said, pointing to the far corner of the restaurant.

"Thanks," I said, scooting out of the booth. As I turned toward the restroom, I was startled by Jackie's stare from her booth. She looked like a cat getting ready to pounce on its prey, eyes narrowed and piercing.

Not knowing what to do, I smiled at Jackie, but she didn't smile back—and that's when I knew. The watchful eyes I'd been feeling all afternoon, walking next to and talking with Izzy, weren't what I'd thought at all.

It'd been her.

chapter 6

SOMEHOW, I'D MADE it through the first week of camp. Now it was Saturday and I was heading to a ghost town, which would have been cool if anything felt cool right then.

"Girls!" Aunt Maureen said excitedly. "Do you know that South Pass City is where women first earned the right to vote?" She turned around in her seat to make intense eye contact with Kennedy in the third row, then me in the middle. "You have these pioneer women to thank for your freedoms."

She faced forward again and read from her phone. "South Pass City had the first female justice of the peace, Esther Hobart Morris." In the side mirror, I saw her look up, then gasp, pointing as we sped by a road sign. "Look! That said that we're on the Wyoming Women's Suffrage Pathway right now. 'Home of the women's vote'!"

"I women's vote we turn around," Kennedy said with a groan. "This drive is taking forever. I'm getting carsick." *Cah-sick.*

"Crack your window," Uncle Bran suggested from the driver's seat.

Kennedy groaned again, loudly. "Suffrage is right."

"That doesn't mean what you think it does, Ken," Uncle Bran said. "Suffrage is the right—"

"Like I care, Brandon," Kennedy interrupted.

"Stop calling him that; he's Dad," her mom said angrily, not looking back this time. "I told you it'd take two hours, and it's been an hour and forty-five minutes. We're almost there. It's going to be fun. And, young lady, you've never been carsick a day in your life."

"What?" Kennedy snapped when I glanced at her.

She put on headphones and scrunched down in her seat with a huff.

Next to me in his booster, Kane was zonked out, snoring softly, his mouth hanging open, his head cranked in a way that didn't seem comfortable. Concerned, I'd pointed it out earlier to Aunt Maureen, but she'd just laughed and told me that younger kids sleep in weird positions.

We were going to the South Pass City Historic Site, which

apparently was part of the Oregon Trail and had a gold mine way back when, but was now just a bunch of abandoned old buildings in the middle of nowhere.

Aunt Maureen had been super excited, and old me might have been okay with it because I don't mind historical stuff and am generally okay with doing things with family. But today I couldn't think of anything I'd rather do *less*. I had a ton on my mind, and Kennedy was way too grumpy for it to be anything other than a disaster.

Not that I said that to Aunt Maureen.

That would have been rude.

"Look at the antelope!" Uncle Bran said, pointing toward the rolling hills on the left side of the car. I saw five white butts bounding over the sagebrush, fleeing into the distance.

"Cool," I said, trying to balance out their own daughter's nastiness, even though we'd seen about fifty antelope on the trip so far, so these weren't exactly special.

Uncle Bran pointing out every antelope in Wyoming was like if I got excited about every seagull on the beach at home.

Colette had loved to watch the seagulls. She'd talk for them in funny voices and name them incompatible names like Bunky and Earl.

I got out my phone and texted my best friend.

I'm not me without you

I felt the notification buzz in my hand, telling me the number was disconnected.

Because your best friend is dead, and you need to deal with it instead of pretending she can still hear you.

We turned off the two-lane highway toward what definitely did *not* look like a city, and there was a literal cowboy waiting for us on a gorgeous speckled gray quarter horse. The cowboy wore a red plaid shirt, blue jeans, boots, and a hat—and was chewing on a piece of grass, making me feel like I was in some sort of Old West documentary.

"I wonder if we can ride," I said quietly, but no one heard me. I missed riding on the beach back home.

"That must be our guide, Denver," Uncle Bran said, waving as we bumped across a dirt parking area. The cowboy tipped his hat.

"His name's *Dallas*," Aunt Maureen said, beaming at the man. "And he's cute!"

"Settle down, missy," Uncle Bran teased. "You're spoken for."

"Said the man with a crush on his hairdresser."

Uncle Bran parked the car, and they lovingly smiled at each other while I squirmed uncomfortably in my seat.

"You guys are gross," Kennedy said.

"Oh, are we?" Uncle Bran said, reaching over and grabbing Aunt Maureen's shoulder and pulling her toward him. "I'll show you gross." He planted a big kiss on her lips.

"Ohmygod," I said, pushing the button to open the sliding door of the minivan and hopping out.

"Undo my belt!" Kane said, kicking his feet, wide awake now. "Undo my belt! I'm stuck! I want out!"

"Me too!" Kennedy said, rushing up from the third row. She expertly undid Kane's seat belt like she'd done it a million times before and quickly kissed his forehead, showing her softer side for an instant before jumping down next to me. "They're the worst."

"Yeah," I agreed, since it was the first thing she'd said to me this whole trip that could be considered conversation.

"I should be on the lake right now, waterskiing with those guys from the general store." She stretched her hands high over her head, staring at the cowboy while her shirt lifted up. I was beginning to understand that showing off her belly button was one of Kennedy's signature moves. "Of course, the scenery is nice here, too."

"It could be worse," I said, hoping she thought I was agreeing with her even though honestly the cowboy's blue roan was more interesting to me than he was.

"Howdy, folks!" he said as we finally made our way over.

"Welcome to the South Pass City Historical Site. I'm Dallas, but you can call me Dally." He patted his horse and said, "This here is Della."

Dallas, who I would not be calling Dally, hopped down and shook everyone's hands, asking their names and repeating them like he was committing them to memory forever.

"Are you a real cowboy, or is that a costume because you don't have a sheriff's badge but maybe you left it at home did you leave it at home?" Kane asked, looking up at Dallas curiously.

Dallas laughed. "Well, I'm not a sheriff," he began.

"Oh," Kane said, disappointed. "What are you, then?"

"I'm a college student studying agriculture."

"What's agg-i-cur . . . What's that?" Kane asked.

"In my case, I'm going to be a food scientist."

Kane looked at him blankly.

"But I grew up on a ranch and do rodeo, so yes, you can call me a cowboy," Dallas added quickly.

Kane seemed satisfied.

Addressing all of us, holding Della's reins loosely as she shifted her weight, Dallas said that he'd take us on a tour around the structures that remained in Old Pass City from the old days, which included the saloon, school, store, and mine.

"Then we'll tour the recently uncovered tunnels at the Carissa Gold Mine—"

"Underground?" I interrupted, not meaning to, touching my fingers to my lips.

"Yes, ma'am, the tunnels cut through the rock," he said. "We'll walk along the original tracks laid by gold miners in the eighteen hundreds by candlelight." I must have looked as horrified as I felt, because he said, "I promise it's safe. We do tours all the time."

"Wicked awesome," Kennedy said, and it sounded like she meant it.

"Yeah," I agreed, despite feeling like locking myself in the minivan.

Dallas led us to a cluster of buildings set against the backdrop of a small hill. We started on the left with the schoolhouse, which was just a single-room log cabin where kids of all ages were taught by one teacher. We had to look at the classroom setup through a glass partition so we wouldn't mess anything up, I guess. Kane smashed his face against the glass and blew; I'm sure it looked funny on the other side of the glass. He left behind a wet smudge that Aunt Maureen didn't notice.

The schoolhouse had a freestanding closet behind it, which Dallas said was the outhouse: otherwise known as a bathroom with no electricity or running water.

"Those kids had it rough," Kennedy said as we walked toward the general store, proving she was paying attention. I tried to, too, but dread was growing in my core. Not only was I afraid of the dark, but I was also afraid of small spaces—and being crushed.

I numbly followed along through several more buildings, not even laughing at Kane leaving his mark on all the glass partitions. Inside the old saloon, zoning out listening to Dallas talk, I caught my reflection in the ancient mirror behind the bar. I saw a hunched-forward teenager, half of her face covered by stringy dark hair, limbs too long, skin too pale.

That girl used to stand a little taller.

That girl used to pull back her hair so you could see her face.

That girl used to feel comfortable in her skin, sometimes.

Oh yeah? That girl was never any good. It was all a lie. She just lived in the glow of Colette's spotlight.

That thing in the mirror? That's the real Tess.

"Is everything okay?" Aunt Maureen whispered. She looked concerned. "Are you having fun?"

"I am," I lied, "but I can't go in the mine. I can't go underground." I braced myself for her to tell me I had to.

"That's okay, Tessy Bear, you can skip that part."

She smiled warmly at me like she didn't care at all, before refocusing on whatever Dallas was saying. But somehow, a half hour later, I ended up blindly following everyone along the ore tracks through the entrance to the tunnel. Aunt Maureen had made it seem like nothing—had told me I didn't have to do it—but for some reason, I went.

It was a mistake.

At first, I could see pretty well, and I felt okay about it. The sun from outside beamed through the opening behind us, and Dallas held a lantern up above his shoulders to guide our way. Kane skipped happily, running his hand along the rock wall. I concentrated on stepping over instead of tripping on the wooden slats that connected the metal tracks.

But then the outside light started to fade, and the walkway felt like it got tighter, the rock walls on both sides of me and the ceiling above leaning in like friends with a serious secret.

I didn't like it; I didn't want to know the secret.

"Is the path getting smaller?" I asked, but Uncle Bran asked a question at the same time, so no one heard me.

I smell another freak-out coming, said my nasty inner self. *Your aunt and uncle are going to be so glad they agreed to let you come on this trip. I mean, is that your heartbeat? Calm down!*

I took a deep breath of air that hadn't seemed stale and stifling before—but did then. I pictured it crawling into my lungs, attaching itself to the sides of my airways all the way down. I took another breath, and I couldn't fill my lungs as much. I tried again, and I got even less air.

"Um . . ." I began, but everyone was loving the tour, talking at once, excitedly bombarding Dallas with questions. Their voices bounced off the walls, traveling deeper and deeper into the hill where I did *not* want to go.

"Workers blasted into the rock in the eighteen hundreds to make this English tunnel," Dallas said. "Now, it's called an English tunnel because—"

I didn't care why. My skin was crawling. We'd gone so far that there was no more outside light at all, and the glow of Dallas's lantern made everything look an eerie red.

As if she were a mind reader, Kennedy turned and said, eyes devilish, "It'd be the perfect setting for a horror movie, wouldn't it?"

I stopped walking. Kennedy and everyone else sauntered on, stopping every so often to look at something Dallas had pointed out. But I was frozen.

"I want to leave," I whispered. My voice wouldn't get loud. I needed to walk forward, to keep up with them, or I'd be left entirely in the dark.

I checked the walls. They were definitely edging closer. I checked the ceiling, noticing that it, too, was—

Someone touched the back of my head.

Gasping, I spun around to check what I already knew: that no one was nearby.

I screamed the loudest and longest I'd ever screamed in my life.

chapter 7

IN MY DREAM, in the dark, I followed Colette down the cabin steps. She didn't hold on at all; she kept looking back to smile encouragingly at me, and it made me nervous she'd lose her balance, but she didn't.

Her red hair was long and loose around her face, her freckles had multiplied, and she wore a T-shirt that said ASK ME ABOUT THE AFTERLIFE.

She danced and spun and skipped across the thin, worn, multicolor-striped carpeting to the back door of the cabin, the space barely lit by the porch light still on in front. Colette walked into flip-flops, then went outside, me following, the gravel crunching under our feet.

She put her hand up to side-block her mouth: whisper pose.

"I met a boy today," she said at a regular volume. She took her hand away. "He's kind of nerdy but so cute!" She did her signature happy shoulder dance. "He's hung up on his old girlfriend, but if he wasn't, I'd be all, 'I volunteer as tribute!'"

I laughed at Colette's reference to the Hunger Games, a series she'd read so many times the covers of the books were duct-taped to the spines.

"Did your mom give away your copies?" I asked Colette in the dream.

She shrugged. "Not yet, but she will."

"Don't you care?"

Colette didn't answer. Instead, she went over and climbed up the two-person rock. I stared at her as she jumped off into the sagebrush. I bet that scratched her ankles, but she didn't seem to mind. She immediately climbed up again, one knee on the rock first, then all of her.

"The boy I met wants to know why no one saved him," she said, looking ahead of her, not at me. She jumped off, her hair flying straight up, landing with a thud. Laughing bitterly, she climbed back up.

"He's pretty mad about that part. Like, where was his dad? Where were his friends? His stupid girlfriend?"

She jumped off again.

"Why are you doing that?" I asked.

She didn't answer; she only climbed the rock.

"I wonder the same thing: why no one saved me."

"We tried! We tried to figure out where you were, but it was too late!"

Her eyes snapped to mine. They were blank, unfriendly. "Did you, *Tess*?"

Jump.

Climb.

"*Frankie* tried to help me," Colette said. "You just went along with it—but not at first. You didn't even *believe* her at first."

Jump.

Climb.

I felt sick because it was true. Frankie had figured out the clues before I had—and believed them—because she saw things that other people didn't sometimes. That *I* didn't. Colette had been playing the game we'd made up as kids, and Frankie had remembered the details and been able to connect them. Without Frankie doing that, the police might *never* have found Colette.

But it's not like I didn't do other things, like hang up posters and try to be there for Colette's parents. And I helped Frankie when she asked me to. I just didn't figure it out on my own.

Because you're book smart but street stupid, Mean Me said, with me even in dreams.

"You were *both* supposed to be my best friends," Colette said.

Jump.

Climb.

"We are!" I said. "I am," I whispered. "I'll always be your best friend."

Colette looked at me again, with those same empty eyes. "Prove it," she said, stepping to the edge of the rock, her flip-flops hanging over the edge. "If you're my best friend, then save me."

She jumped. But this time the ground opened up like a tunnel to the center of the earth, and instead of falling just three or four feet and landing with a thud in the sagebrush, she was swallowed into the darkness.

"Colette!" I screamed, rushing over to peer down into the pit, unable to see or hear her at all. "Colette! Are you there? Colette! Come back! Colette!" I screamed and screamed and sobbed in my dream.

Suddenly, I was awake, Kennedy's hand on my shoulder. I blinked into the darkness, looking for Colette.

"It's okay," Kennedy whispered. "You're okay. You were just dreaming."

I swallowed hard and took a big breath, trying to slow my heartbeat. Kennedy took her hand away, picking up a glass of water on the nightstand. "Here."

I chugged the whole thing, then set down the empty glass.

"Sorry for waking you up," I said.

"Sorry about Colette."

Kennedy flopped back onto her bed, and I rolled over and hugged Woogles, my childhood teddy bear. I spent most of the rest of the night wide awake listening to the noisy crickets—Frankie had been right about them—counting the nails in the logs on the wall, and thinking about the best friend I hadn't been strong enough to save, even in a dream.

chapter 8

"WE CAN TRADE partners if you want."

"Trying to get rid of me?" Izzy joked, making my cheeks turn pink.

It was Monday at camp, the second full week in July. Almost three full months without Colette. Time was just passing without her. Normal things were happening, and I didn't get it.

Like Jackie was flirting with Izzy: normal. She'd tried to get his attention on his way over to my table by calling his name repeatedly with her hand up like she had the answer to an algebra problem. I felt sorry for her and vowed never to be that obvious about a crush.

Izzy and I had been assigned as partners, and Jackie had been paired with Jasmine. Even though I felt comfortable with Izzy, I would have been okay trading if it meant no more glares from Jackie.

"It seems like she likes you," I said. "Maybe you want to . . ."

I didn't know how to end that sentence.

"Are you trying to set me up?" He laughed, making me blush more. Izzy leaned in and said quietly, "I know she likes me. She makes me heart-shaped birthday cakes every year. It's nice but totally embarrassing." It was Izzy's turn to redden. He tugged on his ear a couple times. "I get that she's cute and everything, but she's just kind of a know-it-all, you know? She has the best grades and is the best at art and is the best athlete, and she's just . . ." He glanced around to make sure no one was listening, then leaned in even more. "Jackie's a Veruca."

"A what?"

"Veruca Salt? *Charlie and the Chocolate Factory*?"

Colette had loved that book. She'd hated the movie.

"Oooooh," I said. "That's funny . . . and kinda mean."

"You don't know Jackie," Izzy said, shrugging. "And before you think I'm a jerk, you should know that I've told her I'm not interested. *Nicely. A lot.*"

I looked at Jackie, who was thankfully already working on her project with Jasmine, so she wasn't shooting me dagger eyes. She had on a bright green sundress with a low-cut front that showed off what she had and I didn't. Her hair was perfectly curled down her board-straight back; she had really good posture. My heart tugged for her, liking a guy for forever and him never liking you back. That had to feel crappy.

Straightening my turtle shell, I looked at Izzy. Even though I felt sorry for Jackie, I did like that he hadn't fallen for a girl with a bad personality just because she looked like a Barbie.

I didn't like that she didn't like that he was friends with me, though.

She thinks he likes you, *dummy*, Mean Me said. *So, she's not that* smart, *because there's no way. He's easily the cutest guy here.*

Axl's cuter.

Not even close. Anyway, don't get any ideas, because you're a loser who thinks she's being haunted by her dead best friend, so that makes you a crazy loser. Izzy could never like you, not if he knew the real Tess.

I wanted to shout at the voice in my head that I wasn't even thinking that way about Izzy, that I'd just met him, that I was still too sad about Colette to even think about a boyfriend. But Izzy brought me back to reality.

"So, do you want to draw first, or do you want me to?" he asked, messing with his hair. We were going to spend today and tomorrow on a charcoal drawing project. Karly had lectured on adding detail to faces earlier, and we were supposed to apply what we'd learned. At least drawing portraits was something I could do, and it would keep my brain from spinning about Colette and stop me from demolishing my fingers.

"Draw," I said definitively. "I mean if that's okay?"

He shrugged. "Sure. How do you want me to be?"

While it would be easier to draw his face the way he was sitting now than at a three-quarter angle, he'd be *staring right at me*, and I definitely didn't want that.

"You can just sit normally," I said. "Or, um . . ."

I looked around the classroom to see what other pairs were doing. The room was buzzing as eleven sets of campers chatted quietly, most of them already being productive, except for Axl and a boy named Tim, who were mopping up a cup of water Axl had knocked over. The steady noise of the classroom was occasionally interrupted by the screeching of metal against the labyrinth floor as people shifted in their chairs to get the right angles.

"Oh, uh, I guess just look at your phone," I said.

"Or, if you don't care if I look down, I could read?" Izzy asked, raising his big, dark eyebrows. "I'm toward the end of a book."

"Cool."

I couldn't hide my surprise when he pulled *Artemis Fowl* from his bag. I was glad to see he read more than comics.

"What?" he asked.

"Nothing . . . I'm just . . ." *Surprised you read?*

What a jerkish assumption, said the mean voice in my head. *You think you're the only kid who's ever picked up a book before?*

No, I snapped back. *I don't think that!*

Yes you do!

Izzy looked at me curiously. "Did you want to finish your sent—"

Karly cleared her voice loudly, cutting him off. "Let's get to work, okay?" she said from where she was sitting across from Jake. She gave me and Izzy a stern look.

"Sorry," I said. "We'll start now."

Izzy shifted in his seat, then opened his book to a dog-eared page. I watched his eyes moving left and right as he read, and I felt less anxious with his focus on the book and not on me. I inhaled for four counts, then exhaled for six, like I'd learned from internet advice. It helped, so I did it three more times, as quietly as I could; I didn't want Izzy to think I was some panting weirdo.

Ready to draw, I realized that I'd ripped the corner of my clean paper into strips, so I flipped the page, hoping Izzy hadn't seen.

With my medium pencil, I drew the shape of Izzy's face, wider at the top for his forehead, tapering to a sharp jawline at the bottom. With my lightest pencil, I drew guidelines, splitting the shape in uneven quarters, with more space on the left side than the right since his right side was turned away from me. Then I drew another line to split the bottom half into quarters again.

I started on Izzy's kind of big, straight nose. Noses are challenging for a lot of people, but they've always been easy for me. At least until now.

I hadn't really wanted to draw since Colette's accident, but before that, art had been part of my life for as long as I remembered. I'd taken classes after school and had placed at art competitions in and outside of school. It wasn't like taking three months off would have made me *forget* how to draw or something.

And yet suddenly, I couldn't do it.

The first time I drew Izzy's nose, I couldn't believe what I was looking at.

One of those elephants trained to scribble on paper could do better, Mean Me jeered. *An emoji has better detail than that!*

I felt myself curling back into turtle pose as I used my big eraser to get rid of the horribly embarrassing first attempt. Thankfully, Izzy was so into his book that he didn't see what I'd done. I tried to reset with breathing again, but after drawing, erasing, and redrawing Izzy's nose three more times, I gave up and moved on to his lips. What ended up on the page was a tragic flattened heart. I erased those and drew his eyes, which were reasonable, but when I tried to re-create his eyebrows, it looked like twin porcupines had taken up residence at the top of his face.

Izzy was super normal-looking . . . nice-looking . . . even striking. But I'd made him look like a disaster!

"Ugh!" I said, slamming my notebook shut.

Izzy looked up at me and frowned. "Not going well, huh?"

"I can't draw," I said, frustrated.

"Yeah, digital's more my thing, so I get it," Izzy said, clearly trying to be nice. "It doesn't have to be perfect, though."

"No, that's not what I mean," I said. "Drawing *is* my thing. But I can't . . . I can't do it."

He set his book on the table. "Oh, I get it." He drummed his thumbs on his book a couple times. "You're probably just having an off day. You do seem, you know, maybe not totally focused?" He drummed a couple more times. "Do you want me to draw first? And you can try it again after lunch?"

"Sure," I said. "Thanks."

"Eh?" Izzy asked, holding up his book. A sliver of tension seeped out of my shoulders; he really seemed like a nice person. I agreed, and he slid the book across the table like we were playing air hockey. "Don't lose my place."

"I won't," I said, grateful that I could just sit and read and didn't have to try to draw again right away. The sound of

Izzy's pencil scratching around his sketchbook was relaxing, too.

Before I knew it, I'd read forty pages of *Artemis Fowl* and Karly announced that it was time for lunch.

"Want to see?" Izzy asked. "I'm not finished, but you can check out what I've done so far."

"Okay," I said curiously.

"Okay, don't get mad," Izzy said, turning his sketchbook toward me. "I took a manga class, but I'm not the best."

The girl had oversize eyes, heavy lidded, miniature lakes near the bottom lids. Her eyelashes fanned out like wings, and her neat eyebrows sloped down toward her ears. Izzy hadn't added tons of detail yet but there was dark shading under her eyes and a heart-shaped tear rolling down one of her cheeks. Her lips were pressed together, like she was holding something back. Her hair fell in tiered curtains to her collarbones. Mine was longer, but the center part and neglected layers were right.

The girl in the picture was sad.

The girl looking at the picture was sad.

"The friend I told you about, the one who flipped over on her bike?" I whispered to Izzy. "She was my best friend." I sniffed hard. "She didn't come with me this summer because she died." I paused, staring at the picture. "And now I can't draw anymore."

Izzy looked shocked at first, but just for a second; then he looked sad, too.

"I have candy in my lunch sack," he said. "Follow me."

⁓

IZZY AND I walked around the back side of the library and settled in the grass against the wall. Everyone else was at the picnic tables under the trees on the other side of the building, and I was sure that Jackie was taking note of both Izzy and me being missing.

Izzy yanked at his shorts, then stuck his legs out in front of us, and I checked out his sort-of-nerdy sneakers, which looked like what my mom's boyfriend would wear to work out.

I noticed that my legs were almost as long as his, but his rust-colored Bermuda shorts almost touched his knees and my faded denim shorts were mid-thigh. My feet were at least a couple sizes smaller than his, but my slip-on sneakers were seriously cooler.

"You don't have to, but if you want, you can tell me about your friend," Izzy said, reaching into his zippered lunch bag and pulling out a sandwich wrapped in a reusable wrapper with a bee print. "My mom's full eco," he said, rolling his eyes at the bees. "If you want to make her mad, use a plastic baggie."

"Why would I want to make your mom mad?" I asked.

"Just saying," he said, unwrapping and taking an impressive bite of what looked like a turkey sandwich.

I clutched the top of my crinkled paper sack but didn't open it.

"I was promised candy," I said.

He reached in the bag again and then tossed me a piece of chocolate. I didn't catch it, so it fell in the grass, which embarrassed me.

Of course your reflexes suck.

I picked up the candy but didn't eat it.

"My friend Colette was literally the nicest person I've ever met," I said quietly. "Except not in a *too*-nice sort of way, you know?"

"Sure," Izzy said, covering his full mouth with his hand. "Not fake."

"Right," I said, wondering if I should hold back, if telling Izzy about Colette would come back to bite me in some way. I hoped not, and even though I didn't know him at all, I wanted to tell him. Maybe I just wanted to talk.

"My twin sister, Frankie, and I met Colette in kindergarten," I said. "My sister is kind of an emotional person, and she can be pretty dramatic. She's on the autism spectrum."

Izzy nodded casually, like he knew what that was, and took another huge bite. Half of his sandwich was gone already.

"This one day at school, Frankie was having a meltdown

because she'd made a turtle out of paper scraps and the teacher thought it was trash and threw it away."

"Rude."

"Yeah, I guess. Anyway, Frankie was completely losing it, throwing markers and glue and stuff. I was so embarrassed, I went and stood in the corner and watched. Other kids were screaming because Frankie was scaring them, but Colette just walked over to the trash can and found the turtle and set it on Frankie's desk."

"Awww," Izzy said, "that's rad."

"Did you just say *rad*?" I asked, leaning away from him so I could give him a properly weird look from a distance.

He shrugged and smiled, then popped open a flavored water and chugged some.

I kept telling the story. "When Colette gave back the turtle, it was like someone paused a video, Frankie quieted down so fast. The teacher still sent her to the principal's office."

Izzy laughed. "I did some time there myself." When I raised my eyebrows in question, he said, "I'll tell you another time. Go ahead."

"Anyway, while our teacher was getting everyone settled again, Colette came over to me in the corner. She said, 'I think your sister is okay now. Let's make necklaces.' And that was kind of it. We were just friends after that. And like Frankie *was* okay, being friends with Colette. I mean, it's not like Frankie never got emotional again in her life, but Colette was black-belt-level good at seeing the thing that Frankie needed to calm her down—better than me even sometimes, and I know Frankie pretty well."

I looked at my hands; I'd set down the lunch sack and had been tearing off pieces of skin while I'd been talking. I looked at Izzy, and it seemed like he was trying *not* to look at my hands—maybe to not embarrass me.

I decided to just ignore the wreckage of my fingers and finish the story.

"The three of us loved making up games, and there was this one called dare-or-scare, where you had to do a dare or get a scare," I said. "Colette and I both loved scary stuff, and Frankie loved dares, so we all liked the game."

"Scary movies are killer," Izzy said, starting in on some chips. "Continue."

"Fast-forward to this last school year," I said. "Frankie and Colette had a falling-out." I paused, thinking of Frankie overhearing Mia and Colette talking about her, calling her *tornado brain* because of Frankie's obsession with tornadoes. And maybe because of the way she processes things, I don't know. It hurt my heart to think about how Frankie must have felt, hearing her best friend talk about her behind her back.

I didn't get into all of that with Izzy. Instead, I said, "Colette had done something wrong, and Frankie had gotten mad, and suddenly, they weren't friends anymore. And

I didn't know what to do because that was my sister and my best friend, so I just didn't say anything to either of them about it. I wish I had, because maybe it would have changed things."

Izzy set down his chips and looked at me seriously, listening intently.

"Three months ago, I guess Colette decided to make videos of herself playing dare-or-scare as like a way to apologize to Frankie, since that was all of our thing, but Frankie really loved it the most," I said. "We don't know for sure that's why she did it, since she had an accident doing one of the dares, but that's what my sister and I think." I looked down at the grass and said the last part fast. "Colette lost control and rode her bike into a ravine. The police didn't find her for three days. She died in the hospital."

"Holy . . ."

"I know."

We sat there a long time, the summer breeze floating through, birds chirping at each other. I could hear the rest of the campers laughing loudly as they finished their lunches. I stared at a big, fluffy dandelion sticking up taller than the others, perfect for making wishes.

I wish you hadn't played the game alone.

I wish you weren't terrible at riding bikes.

I wish you were here.

"Do you want my number?" Izzy interrupted my thoughts. It was an awkward thing to say, and he said it awkwardly. "I mean like it's almost time to go back in . . . so in case you want to talk more later or just . . . I don't know. That was weird."

I couldn't help it: I laughed. "It *was* kind of weird," I agreed. *But also nice.* I unlocked my phone and handed it to him. "Here."

Half smiling, he created a new contact for himself, then handed back the phone. I texted him a silly-eyed emoji.

"Now you have mine, too."

chapter 9

UNCLE BRAN HAD done a work meeting from one of the private rooms you can rent in the library, so he was the one who drove me home that day. We walked in the cabin to find Kennedy watching reality TV and eating licorice upside down. Her head was hanging off the muted-plaid couch, the longer part of her hair skimming the floor. The backs of her legs were against the back of the couch, her bare feet straight up in the air.

She looked like one of those '80s pop singers my mom's boyfriend liked, with her half-shaven hair, netted tank top, destroyed high-waisted jean shorts, and bracelets going up both wrists.

I fell into the chair with the white background and terracotta cowboy pattern on it. The furniture here was scratchy, musty, and mismatched, with deflated, uncomfortable cushions. I liked it anyway.

Kane sat on the carpet in front of his sister, playing a game I'd never heard of called pick-up sticks.

"Is this what you've been doing all afternoon?" Uncle Bran asked.

"Basically," Kennedy said.

"Ken, you need to take advantage of being here. You can watch TV anywhere. I thought you were going hiking with Mom and Kane. What happened to that plan?"

"It's hardly a hike if a preschooler can do it."

"Still."

"I didn't feel like it, Brandon."

"Yes, but . . ." Uncle Bran seemed to decide he didn't feel like arguing with his daughter. "Where is Mom, anyway?" he asked, going over and pouring himself some orange juice.

"Maureen's taking a nap," Kennedy said.

"Where's Kane?"

"I have no idea," Kennedy said, winking at her brother.

"Daddy, I'm right here," Kane said.

"Where?" Uncle Bran asked, looking around and pretending not to see him.

"Right here!" Kane shouted from the floor.

"Right here?" Uncle Bran said, suddenly rushing over and picking him up by the waist, then flipping him upside down, making my smallest cousin laugh and squeal.

"I can't hear the show!" Kennedy protested.

I got up and started toward the stairs, wanting some alone time. Kennedy cranked the TV, and Kane's giggles got even louder.

"Tess, we're going to eat at the brewery tonight," Uncle Bran called when I was almost to the loft. "Be ready to go at five!"

"Okay," I said before taking three steps and face-planting onto the bed.

Just as I'd gotten comfortable, I heard talking through the open window that I realized was my aunt. Apparently, she wasn't asleep, and her window in the room underneath ours was open, too. That's how I heard her say:

"I know, I'm just worried about Tess."

I couldn't hear whoever she was talking to, but I suspected it was my mom. My hunch was confirmed seconds later.

"Sis, you haven't seen her fingers. She's mutilating them! I'm sick with worry about my goddaughter." She paused as my stomach clenched into a fist. I moved closer to the window for better eavesdropping. "I know, but I think she needs to see someone."

She listened; I held my breath.

"I'm doing what I can. I'll send you this article I saw online about self-harm as a way to get relief from extreme anxiety or to feel more in control," Aunt Maureen said. "What if she starts *cutting herself*? Or worse?"

My face went hot.

I'd never told anyone. I never would.

Two days after Colette's funeral, I'd pressed a razor blade against my thigh. I hadn't broken the skin or anything, but I'd thought about it. I'd wanted to do it, but I'd started shaking so badly that I could barely hold the blade and then I felt like I was going to throw up. I hadn't done it again since. But still, I couldn't pretend it hadn't happened.

"I know she's a worrier, but it's more than that now. I think she—"

She got quiet; I bit my fingernail.

"Sissy, I know she's your kid. And I know Frankie's a lot to handle. I don't want to make you mad. I just think—"

She listened some more; I pressed my ear against the dirty screen, not wanting to miss a thing.

"Of course, I know you love them! You live for those girls!" Aunt Maureen sighed. "Listen, let's just keep in touch about it. I'll keep watching her here, and you can decide what you want to do when she gets home." She paused and added, "You know what I think. I can even do some research if you don't have time with the inn and Frankie and every—" Pause. "Okay, that's fine."

She waited a few seconds and said, "You're welcome. And I love you, too. Hugs to Charles and Frankie. Bye."

AN HOUR LATER, we sped toward town in the minivan, country music blasting this time, since Uncle Bran said we needed to "embrace the spirit of the West."

Kane was happily dancing in his booster seat, kicking his feet and flapping his hands. Next to him, Kennedy had her arms crossed and was angrily staring out the window as the singer sang about the love of his life: his pickup truck. Aunt Maureen and Uncle Bran sang along at the top of their lungs.

I saw the overpass coming up fast and held my breath.

The day blinked as we went under.

I spun around in my seat to check.

Nothing.

You're so weird!

When I faced forward again, Kennedy was staring at me.

"Why do you do that?" she asked, maybe with less punch than usual.

I shook my head.

"I don't know."

chapter 10

FRIDAY, WE STARTED our photography unit. We'd finished our drawing unit a day early, and there was a street fair happening in town that Karly said would be a good opportunity for interesting pictures. Maybe she just wanted to go to the fair.

I was out of my comfort zone, since the only photography experience I had was taking selfies and stuff on my phone. I had no idea how to work the heavy and awkward loaner camera, but I was okay with taking a break from drawing.

Because you're horrible at it.

Somehow, I'd managed to finish my sketch yesterday, even though it only slightly resembled Izzy. Real Izzy had been sweet, but the drawing was awful.

"Say feta," Izzy said, pointing his camera at me and making me blush.

Snap.

Across the room, Jackie shook her head and whispered something to a girl that looked a lot like her, just with darker blond hair. Jackie was clearly annoyed that Izzy was taking my picture instead of hers.

"Izzy, stop," I said quietly, wanting him to cut it out so Jackie would quit scowling at me. "You're embarrassing me."

"Okay, sorry," he said, shrugging before turning in his seat and aiming the camera at other kids instead. He and Girl Sam took pictures of each other taking pictures of each other, laughing. Everyone was trying out their loaners; I didn't even remember where we were supposed to put the dial.

Karly had talked to us about terms like ISO and aperture—words I knew I'd never remember—and the rule of thirds. We learned that meant mentally dividing the scene into thirds, both up and down and side to side. Where those imaginary dividing lines crossed, that was where the important thing in the picture should go, like someone's eyes or a house in the distance.

I knew I probably wouldn't be able to take pictures of people, because no one was going to stand still long enough for me to figure out whether I was following or violating the rule of thirds. I figured I'd just point the camera at whatever and hope for the best.

Now we were leaving to walk around town again and try the cameras outside.

"Green River Rendezvous starts today," disheveled Jake said, matter-of-fact. We were walking through the library toward the front door, and I hadn't noticed him next to me. "The street fair is the first event. There will be a lot of people. Let's be partners."

I looked around at the other kids, then back at Jake. "Did Karly tell us to have partners?"

"No." Jake's greasy hair was over his glasses, and as usual, he looked like he'd slept in his clothes. He walked through the heavy outside door and dropped it on me instead of holding it so I could take it. "A lot of people go to Rendezvous. It'll be loud."

I understood that maybe Jake wanted someone by his side because he wasn't comfortable with crowds. I looked around for Izzy, not getting why Jake had chosen me, but feeling okay with being there for him. He was nice, and besides, I'd want someone to do that for Frankie if she was having a hard day.

"What's Green River Rendezvous?" I asked, struggling to keep up with him on the sidewalk, close enough so we could hear each other but not too close to bug him. I already knew that Jake had personal space issues from when he wouldn't let anyone sit next to him at the Mexican restaurant; I did not yet know that he was really into Wyoming history.

"Rendezvous started in 1825," he said quickly in a monotone voice, like a fast-talking robot. He somewhat reminded me of Frankie, except she'd gotten better at changing the tone of her voice in the last couple years.

Jake kept talking as we followed everyone else.

"At the first Green River Rendezvous, mountain men and Native Americans met and traded fur and weapons to get ready for winter. They had fun together, so they kept meeting every year. We still celebrate Rendezvous during the second full weekend in July. You're lucky you're here. There's a street fair today, a parade tomorrow, and a rodeo all weekend. I don't like the fair or the parade. The best part is the reenactment. They dress up and charge in on their horses. It's cool."

"It sounds cool," I said.

"It is," Jake said, like the Rendezvous's coolness was flat-out fact. "You should go this weekend. I'm going."

"Maybe I will," I said, not really wanting to go to a rodeo, a reenactment, or a parade. Not wanting to do anything.

"I wish we had camp at night, because then I could take pictures of the stars."

"Camp at night," I said. "Huh."

"Everything is better at night."

Except that's when the nightmares happen.

I'd had the same dream, Colette jumping off the boulder and then tumbling into nothing, three times now.

We'd reached the part of Pine where the street fair started. Temporary red-and-white fences had been placed at the ends of the three-block stretch to keep traffic out, and there were vendors selling all sorts of things from art to jewelry to food to toys. Seemingly the whole town of Pinedale was packed into the three blocks.

"Wow," I said. "You're right. That is a lot of people!"

"They come from Boulder, Cora, Daniel, Big Piney, and even Jackson. Rendezvous is cool."

"So you said." I smiled, but he wasn't making eye contact to see it.

"Let's take pictures from the bench," Jake said, starting off toward the sidewalk on the right. Even though we didn't have to have partners—and technically I could go where I wanted—I felt the pull of an invisible string and followed him anyway.

"Are you sure you don't want to go down the center of the street?" I asked, thinking we'd get better pictures.

"No." Jake was clearly stubborn. He also clearly didn't want to touch anyone else.

I decided to make the best of it. On the sidewalk, Jake climbed up on the bench, and I did, too. Since we were basically at the corner of the giant rectangle of people that was the fair, we had a decent aerial view. Jake and I both took a few pictures before I hopped down, randomly shooting into the crowd from a different angle, like Karly had told us to.

"Make sure your subject is in focus," Karly said, appearing behind me, startling me. "And, Jake?" she said. "Are you doing okay?"

"I'm fine," Jake said flatly before gesturing in my direction. "This girl is my partner."

I wasn't offended that Jake hadn't remembered my name. My sister sometimes didn't remember people's names either, people she'd been in class with all year or seen regularly.

Karly smiled at me. "It's nice that you two are working together."

"Thanks," I said. She left to check on other campers.

"Can I take a picture of you?" I asked.

"Yes," Jake said, jumping down from the bench with a *thunk* and standing in front of me so the empty part of the street was behind him.

"Will you move over here, actually?" I asked, half expecting him to say no, but he moved so the crowd was behind him.

I looked through the viewfinder and pictured the invisible gridlines, then positioned Jake's right eye where I imagined the upper right intersection would be. I twisted the lens back and forth until Jake's face seemed to be in focus.

The crowd behind him was a blur of shapes and colors, just what Karly might consider "visual interest."

I took a few shots of Jake standing there, not looking at me, probably thinking of mountain men and Native Americans or taking pictures of stars at night, seeming comfortable being just as he was.

With the camera in front of my face, adjusting dials I knew nothing about, snapping pictures I was sure would be blurry and unusable, I smiled even though Jake didn't.

I wished I were a little more like him.

A little more comfortable as I was.

———

BACK AT CAMP, after lunch under the trees outside the library, we returned to the meeting room with the labyrinth floor. Karly explained that we'd go in three groups of eight to the library computers and look through our pictures, then choose one we liked the best to edit and have printed for our portfolios. The people who weren't on the computers were supposed to start thinking about their "special projects."

"I want you to come up with an art piece that you can keep working on for the rest of camp, whenever you have time," Karly said. "It can be in whatever style you want—and about anything you want. Just pick something meaningful to you. We'll do an art show at the end of the summer and display your special projects in addition to some of the other works.

"Today, when it's not your turn on the computers, I want you to fill out a worksheet," Karly said, prompting a few groans around the room. "It's just for you, not to turn in, but I hope it'll help each of you come up with a great idea for your special project. I can't wait to see what you create!"

Karly looked over at the students on the side of the room near the door. "Everyone in the first two rows, follow me to the computers." To the rest of us, she said, "Everyone else, grab a worksheet off my desk and start brainstorming!"

Jackie and two of her friends, and five other kids I didn't know, left with Karly.

"Can my special project be taking a nap?" Axl asked Jasmine, resting his head on his arm on top of his art table.

Jake turned around in his seat in the front row. "No, it has to be an art project," he said seriously.

"Duh, Jake," said a really tall kid in the back row, with red hair that stuck out under a trucker hat with a fish on it. He laughed in a mocking way and added, "He's not an *idiot*."

"Axl looks pretty serious about napping," Izzy cut in.

"I am," Axl muttered, his eyes closed. "Everyone hush."

"I think Jake was right to explain it to him," Izzy said.

The redhead rolled his eyes, sitting back in his chair and

crossing his arms over his chest. "You're always sticking up for him, Kosta. What, is he your boyfriend?"

Two other boys laughed.

Boy Sam cleared his throat and shifted in his seat uncomfortably. I remembered that he was getting to know all of these kids, just like I was. He and I shared a nervous glance.

"We're not boyfriends," Jake said flatly, eyes on the worksheet he'd already started. "We're neighbors, and Izzy is heterosexual. I know this because he likes—"

"Okay now!" Izzy said loudly, interrupting Jake and standing up, his cheeks reddening. He went to Karly's desk and got the pile of papers, then began handing them out to everyone but Jake. "Let's just do the stupid worksheets."

———

WHEN IT WAS my group's turn on the computer, I clicked through the pictures I'd taken at the fair. The ones from the bench were okay, but the best were the ones of Jake. I deleted all the pictures where he had his eyes closed or his mouth open and was left with three. Karly told us to enlarge the image to check focus, so I did. One was blurrier than the other two, and in another, I could see myself reflected in Jake's glasses. I'd narrowed down the options and chosen the best.

"That's the one you're using for your portfolio?" Boy Sam asked, nodding toward my monitor. He had a close-up of ice cream on his.

"What do you think?"

"It's a cool picture," Boy Sam said. "It looks like an ad for glasses or . . ."

"White T-shirts?" I asked. We both smiled. "Thanks, I like yours, too," I said, meaning it. I wouldn't have thought to take a close-up picture of something as regular as ice cream. "The texture is interesting."

Uh, what? Mean Me butted in. *Stop trying to sound like you know what you're talking about.*

"Thanks, Tess," Boy Sam said happily. We both refocused on our work.

I started applying filters to make the colors in the street-fair scene behind Jake super bright, because I thought Karly would like that. Compared to the plain colors Jake had on—tan shorts and a white T-shirt—I thought it could be a good contrast. Feeling like maybe I was getting the hang of it, I enlarged the picture again to take a closer look at what I'd done. Left to right, the street party was a sea of color.

A woman wore a purple dress.

There were one . . . two . . . three plaid shirts under out-of-focus faces.

A girl's white-blond hair blew back in the breeze.

The boy she was talking to wore a stark black T-shirt.

And . . .

There he was.

Between two small clusters of people, but not with either of them, stood the man in the now sunshine-yellow scarf, thanks to the filters I'd applied. Even though the scene was blurred, I could easily see that he wasn't chatting with a friend, buying something, or eating food. I could easily see that he was alone, facing forward, staring straight ahead.

Staring right into the camera.

Or at the girl behind it.

chapter 11

"Hey, Mom," I said quietly.

I was on the boulder at the side of the cabin, which I now thought of as Colette's. I sat in my spot, leaving room for her, smelling of bug spray and sleep breath.

"Hey, my girl," my mom said, quietly, too. My heart felt like it'd been filled with warm water, hearing her voice. I could see she was at the four-person kitchen table in the cottage by the inn, white cabinets behind her, café curtains blowing in the ocean breeze. "I'm glad you called. I've been missing my Tess."

I'd talked to my mom on video chat only once since I'd been here; Charles had been on, too. It'd been cut short because a guest had fallen down in the lobby. Mom had checked in over text every day, not that our short strings were like a real conversation.

Not that I was real with her.

"So, how are you?" Mom asked, looking concerned. Her dark, straight hair that matched mine except for the gray in hers was up in a messy knot, and she had on her fluffy gray bathrobe. "Aunt Maureen is worried about you."

"I'm fine," I said automatically. My mom tilted her head to the side like she didn't believe me and waited for me to say more. "Camp is cool." *Except for the jealous Barbie.* "I'm learning to take pictures." *Including one with a stalker in it.* "It's fun being back in Pinedale." *Except when I go under the overpass or have nightmares every night.*

"Well, all that sounds great," Mom said, looking relieved. She hesitated, then asked, "How are your fingers?"

I shrugged. "Okay. I mean I get nervous about meeting new people." *And the internet says I have anxiety, which you somehow refuse to see.*

"I know you do," she said. "But have you met some nice new friends?"

"A few, yeah." *None who could ever come close to replacing Colette.* "How are you guys?"

"Oh, things are pretty normal around here," Mom said before taking a sip of the coffee in front of her. "We're booked solid this weekend because there's a beach wedding, so of course your sister chose yesterday to become hyper-irritable and start . . ."

I stopped listening.

A door slammed nearby; I looked around at the neighboring houses: a well-maintained trailer house on the left; a long, single-story house with a horse barn behind; and a pristine, two-story house on the right that was made of the same type of interlocking logs as ours but could never be considered a cabin.

There was no one outside but three hunting dogs, an obsidian cat, and a chestnut horse. Oh, and the horseflies.

I smacked at one on my leg, but it got away. I must have missed that spot with the repellent.

"Speak of the devil," my mom said, seconds before Frankie appeared behind her, putting bunny ears on our mom. Mom turned around and said, "Would you like to say hi to your sister?"

"Are eggs ready?" Frankie asked.

Mom sighed and stood up, then bent down so her face was close to the camera. "I love you, Tess. Try to relax, okay?"

Has anyone ever relaxed when they were told to relax?

"Sure, okay," I said. "I love you, too."

Frankie rarely told my mom, or anyone, that she loved them. Maybe that was why I felt like I *always* needed to say it back, even when I didn't really feel like saying it myself.

Mom blew a kiss at the phone and went over to the fridge

to get eggs. Frankie picked up the phone and walked back to the bedroom we used to share as kids, before we each took a room inside the inn when we got too old to share.

It'd been my idea.

I'd needed some space.

"There was a tornado near Hot Springs, Wyoming, yesterday," Frankie said before flopping down on her childhood bed.

"I don't know where that is," I said, biting my pinkie fingernail.

"Hold on." The video paused and the screen got blurry; then she came back. "It's three hours and forty minutes from you driving, not that tornadoes stay on roads." Frankie paused and added, "It was just a small one, and no one was hurt."

"Ah." I didn't know what to say about that. "How's Kai?"

Frankie and Kai had been friends since elementary school. He was a sweet guy who liked to skateboard and who'd crushed on Frankie practically since they met. I think she only realized it a few months ago, right around when Colette went missing.

My sister shrugged, holding the phone straight out in front of her and pushing her face back into the pillow to make herself have a double chin, then touching the rolls with her fingers. "Kai's Kai."

"Is he your boyfriend now?" I asked carefully.

Frankie looked at the camera instead of herself for a second and made her chin normal again. "Kai's my *friend*," she said, a sparkle in her eye that told me he was probably more than a friend, but she wasn't going to talk about it. "Do you like that guy? The one who has a name like a girl?"

I hadn't told Frankie about Izzy; mostly we'd just texted about internet quizzes and this new game she was obsessed with and trying to get me to play.

"How do you know about him?" I asked.

Frankie smiled slyly. "Kennedy."

"You talked to *Kennedy*?" I asked, surprised.

"Sure." Frankie wasn't one for detail.

"Like, do you text? Or video chat? And how often?"

Frankie made a face. "You sound like Mom." She rolled over in bed and said, "We've texted since last year. She said you told everyone at dinner about people you'd met at camp and it was so obvious you liked the boy with the girl's name."

"His name is Izzy, which can be a boy's name, too, and I like him as a *friend*."

My cheeks turned pink, and Frankie put the phone really close to her face, so I could only see one eye and part of her nose.

"You're lying," she said flatly. "Send me a picture."

"I'm not going to take a picture of him!" I said, squishing down into my shoulders, embarrassed. "And there's this other girl who likes him. They go to school together. She—"

"Are you still afraid of the old man?" Frankie interrupted, yawning.

Stop interrupting me! I shouted at her in my head, but not out loud. It sucked when she switched gears like that, but I didn't have the energy to say anything.

"Actually, yeah," I said. "We had to take pictures at camp, and he was in the background of one of mine, staring at me." I paused and lowered my voice. "I think he's stalking me."

"Find him and ask him why," Frankie said, like it was nothing to just track down a scary person and demand to know something.

"I'd never do that," I said.

"I would."

"I know."

I'd thought about telling Aunt Maureen or Uncle Bran, but they'd have told my mom. I didn't want her to freak out and make me go home. And I didn't want her to *not* freak out and brush it off and make me feel like an idiot either.

Frankie got up and grabbed a notebook from the desk, plus a pen with a fuzzy ball stuck to the end. Sitting cross-legged on the bed, with the phone propped up on the pillow, she started writing something.

"Do you want to get off the phone?" I asked.

"I want a picture of Izzy," Frankie said, her eyes on her notebook. "And I want you to have fun. I want Colette to be alive. And I want another tornado to hit our town, not to do damage, but just so I can see it. But I want Colette back the most because it's not fair we were fighting when she died."

Her wandering commentary threw me off—mostly the part about Colette. Where other people tiptoed around the subject, using soft tones and words, Frankie just stomped through it, matter-of-fact, talking about Colette and her death like she'd talk about going to the arcade. It was unsettling. But it might have also been okay. It was better than "I'm sorry for your loss."

"I'm sorry you were fighting when she died," I said sincerely. "That must feel awful."

"Box," Frankie said.

"Okay," I said. "What?"

"I put my feelings in a box."

"I don't know what you're . . ." I furrowed my eyebrows in confusion.

"You asked if I'm sad—or why I'm not sadder—about Colette," she explained. I *had* asked her that . . . two weeks ago. That's Frankie: she'll answer a question someone asked a long time ago without any context, like she doesn't live according to the same concept of time as everyone else. She went on. "I am sad. I miss her all the time. But I put my feelings in a box."

I thought she was being oddly deep and talking about a box in her brain or something, but then she said, "I stole the shoebox in your closet."

Of course she meant a literal box. *My* literal shoebox.

"Did you dump out my hair ties?"

She ignored me. "I write down whatever I'm feeling about Colette and put it in the box. Then I just . . . keep doing life."

I couldn't help it: it choked me up. Tears stung my eyes. I sniffed hard to stop them from falling.

"Gabe told me to do it," Frankie said.

"It's a really good idea," I said, jealous that she had someone like Gabe to give her good ideas for dealing with her emotions.

"I'm going to burn the box at the end of the summer." She laughed. "Gabe didn't tell me to do that part, but Kai saw some video on Viewer about someone burning stuff they write down to release the past or whatever. Kai's weird."

Her expression said she liked Kai's type of weird.

"Izzy's weird, too," I said.

We looked at each other for a few seconds, smiling, acknowledging what we weren't saying out loud. We both liked boys, and neither of us wanted to talk about it.

"Eggs!" I heard Mom call.

Frankie looked at the door, then back at the screen.

"Send the picture," Frankie bossed. "Find the man."

"No to both," I said.

"Yes." She hung up before I could reply.

chapter 12

WEDNESDAY OF THE third week of camp, we met at the rec center instead of the library. It was a field trip day with no art; it was just supposed to be fun.

I walked into the lobby with the hairs standing up on my arms like they had been since we'd driven under the animal bridge. I had no idea why that thing bugged me so much.

I had on a red-and-white-striped one-piece under my red tank top and cutoff shorts, and the suit was riding up. I'd probably grown two inches since the last time I'd worn it. I felt awkward and nervous and generally off.

"You need a wristband," Jackie said with disdain when she saw me looking around, clueless. She was the only other person in the lobby, and she didn't have to talk to me, but she did.

She had a towel wrapped around her body, and I could see rainbow swimsuit straps on her shoulders. Her toenails were painted rainbow colors, too. She rolled her eyes and gestured to the front desk, then looked me up and down, frowning. "You have to *shower* before you get in the water."

She walked through doors that had a sign over them that said POOLS.

I passed the rock-climbing wall on my way to the front desk; there was a man who'd almost reached the top of the wall, and I had to look away even though he had a spotter on the ground. That was something Colette and Frankie would have tried, not me.

"I'm here with the art camp," I said quietly to the college-age student behind the desk. The lobby was humid and smelled like chlorine.

"Sure sure, what's your name?" he asked.

"Tess Harper?"

He looked at a computer screen for long enough to make me think that someone had forgotten to add me to the list.

That's because you're forgettable, the voice in my head cut me down.

Just when I was ready to text Aunt Maureen to come back and get me, the kid said, "Here you are!"

He snapped a hot pink plastic band snugly on my left wrist.

"Shower before and after you use the pools," the kid said. "Hit pound three times to set the code for your locker. No running in the pool area." He raised his eyebrows at me like he was wondering why I was still standing there. "That's it."

I hoisted up my beach bag and followed the signs to the locker room. I got out my towel, then took off everything but my suit and flip-flops, set the code, and locked my locker. I rinsed off under the harsh spray of the shower, trying not to get my hair too wet in the process. My flip-flops were soaked and slippery when I stepped out; I wrapped my beach towel tightly around me and went to join the others.

This place had been under renovation last year, so it was all new to me. In the area before me was a massive, kidney-bean-shaped pool with one part a lazy river, one part a submarine toy for toddlers, and one part a three-story waterslide.

"Tess, we're over here!" Girl Sam yelled from the top of the waterslide, jumping up and down and waving. She was wearing a black bikini that showed off her curvy body, a suit I'd never be comfortable in. "Watch!" she called, her voice echoing through the cavernous space.

Girl Sam backed up and took a couple quick steps, then jumped and shot down the slide. Lying flat, she sped around the first corner, her body flying up so high I worried she'd be launched over the side. Instead, she just gently slid back down. I bit my nail; Girl Sam screamed happily. She wound around three more turns, then shot out of the bottom into the pool below, emerging laughing, her drenched hair stuck to her face.

I walked over to where Boy Sam and Izzy were doubled over laughing, too, waiting for Girl Sam. I got there just as she climbed out of the water; the lifeguard appeared.

"I told you already, no running starts," the angry-looking girl said.

"Sorry," Sam said. "Won't happen again." She smiled at all of us.

"This is your last warning," the lifeguard said before walking away.

"Busted!" Izzy said. He looked at me. "Hey, Tess. You're up!"

"Uh . . ."

"It's fun!" Boy Sam said.

"He did it backward last time," Girl Sam said, pointing at Boy Sam. "It was lit." She pulled her hair over her shoulder and wrung it out like a towel. "Just stay loose, and you'll be fine."

"Okay," I said, not wanting a turn but not wanting them to think I was chicken either.

"I'll hold your towel," said Girl Sam, reaching for it. Reluctantly, I handed it over.

Walking to the steps that led to the slide, Mean Me showed up.

Your suit is up your butt right now and Izzy can see! Gross!

You're going to forget to inhale at the bottom and drown in front of everyone.

Why are you doing this instead of just saying you don't want to? What a pathetic wimp! Stand up for yourself!

With every step up the slide, my knees grew weaker. I was afraid of heights, afraid of drowning, afraid of everything. I felt like I might throw up my breakfast, and the fear of throwing up got in line with the other fears. By the time I made it to the top, my heart was pounding and my palms were clammy. I considered going back down the steps, but then I saw Izzy's huge, excited smile.

"No running starts," the lifeguard said sternly. "Or jumping."

"You don't have to worry about that," I said.

"Go, Tess!" Izzy shouted, and the Sams cheered.

I looked out over the lazy river. Some of the other kids from camp were looking up at me, too, including Jackie, who was lying on a lounge chair in a rainbow bikini. My one-piece felt like a snowsuit compared to what all the other girls were wearing.

I'd bought this suit with Colette last summer. She'd had the same one in purple. We'd loved them so much.

Why aren't you here right now?

"More kids are coming up," the lifeguard said. "You need to go."

"Okay," I said, stepping to the edge. Gripping a handrail, I sat down, legs out in front of me, water rushing under them.

"Want a push?" the lifeguard asked, probably thinking I wouldn't go without one. I might not have.

"Sure," I said, *sure* I would die shortly.

And before I had another second to think about it, I was speeding down the slippery slide, water making my suit ride even higher up my backside, struggling to stay loose like Girl Sam had. Anything but loose, when the force of the first corner came, I flew up in the air like Sam, but instead of gently sliding back down, I landed hard, my head hitting the wet plastic with a thunderous *thud* that echoed everywhere. Two or three seconds later, I was thrust underwater, flailing and trying to feel for the bottom of the pool so I could push back up and breathe. The chlorine felt like acid poured onto the dozens of wounds on my fingers.

Surfacing from the water, I pushed my hair from my face and looked at my fellow campers, expecting laughter and cheers. Instead, I saw concern.

"Are you okay?" Izzy asked.

"Ohmygod, Tess, did you knock yourself out?" Girl Sam asked.

"That was *loud*," Boy Sam said, an exaggerated frown on his face.

The only laughter came from the other end of the pool area, where Jackie and her friends huddled together, losing it at my expense.

"I'm fine," I said, trying to brush it off. "That's how we do waterslides where I'm from. The louder the better."

What the heck are you even saying right now? Do you have a concussion, freak?

As covertly as I could while moving toward the steps, I pulled my suit from my rear and made sure the top was in place, too. On dry land, Girl Sam handed me my towel. I quickly wrapped it around my body.

"Lazy river, then?" Izzy asked, and the rest of us quickly agreed.

For the next two hours, the four of us—sometimes six or seven when Jasmine, Axl, and Jake joined in—floated on noodles, tried to race each other going in the opposite direction that the river was flowing, and tried to race each other swimming with flippers in the right direction, which felt like being an actual fish. Even though I had a lump on my head from the slide and Jackie made it obvious that she was talking about me the whole time, I had a better morning than I'd had in a while.

After lunch of hot dogs and salty chips, Karly gave us the choice of swimming more in the afternoon or using the other facilities at the rec center. We had to put our name on a list next to what we were going to do. The options were Ping-Pong, video games, basketball, or wall climbing.

The Sams, Jasmine, and Jake signed up to climb. A bunch of kids I hadn't talked to wrote their names under *basketball*. Jackie and friends told Karly they wanted to stay in the pool area, because the patio was open now and they could sunbathe. Axl and Izzy signed up for Ping-Pong, but by the time I got the sheet, there was an even number of names, so I wouldn't have a partner. I decided to play video games, even though it wasn't as much of my thing. But at least I could do it alone.

Walking to the shower area, I thought maybe I'd text Frankie if there was an online multiplayer game, to see if she wanted to play. That would make her happy, and making her happy usually made me feel better.

There was a line for the showers, so I left the locker room in search of a drinking fountain. Swimming and the salty lunch had made me thirsty.

I found a water fountain at the end of the hallway, but it had an OUT OF ORDER sign, so I decided to try the one on the second floor. I trudged up the stairs in my clammy flip-flops; it was muggy and even hotter up here, the pool making the whole building swamplike. The second floor had a bunch of classrooms and meeting rooms, but it didn't seem like anything was happening today. I walked by signs outside empty rooms that said KNIT WITS, DRIVER'S ED, CITY COUNCIL, and CHILDBIRTH 101.

When I got to the end, there wasn't a water fountain at all.

Sighing, I went back to the stairwell, then decided to try the top floor.

When I pushed through the double doors, it was even hotter and muggier, and the hallway lights were out. It wasn't dark, but dim. I tried the light switch, but nothing happened. I waved my hands in front of it, and jumped around, in case it would turn on with one of those motion sensors.

Looking up and down the gloomy hallway, I considered how badly I wanted a drink. My mouth felt practically glued shut, so I decided to go for it, hoping the line at the showers would be gone by the time I got back to the locker room.

I forced myself to walk casually by the empty rooms, since there was absolutely nothing wrong, even though I was tense and the slapping noise my flip-flops made on the linoleum made me want to take them off and tiptoe. Irrationally, I wanted to be quiet, so as not to disturb . . .

What? You could turn a carnival into a nightmare.

At the end of the hall, not only was there a drinking fountain, but it was working. Relieved, I leaned over and started chugging like I'd been trapped in the desert for a week. The crisp water was just what I needed. I felt it making its way through my body, cooling me off.

I stood up and wiped my mouth on the back of my hand, feeling refreshed, glad I'd come up here, wondering what temperature they kept the water at because I was a lot cooler than I'd been all day. A lot cooler than I'd been just a minute or two ago.

I was cold, actually.

The fairies clawed up my spine.

I flipped around, expecting . . . who knows what. Nothing—no one—was there.

But it *felt* like someone was.

I froze for a few seconds, waiting. Hesitating.

I took off running toward the stairwell.

Tears sprung into my eyes as I ran, the sound of flip-flops echoing off the walls, floor, and ceiling. I was convinced that someone was behind me, chasing me, reaching out to grab my wet hair and yank me backward. I felt them.

"No, please," I whispered as I ran. "Go away. You're scaring me."

At the doorway to the stairwell, I didn't stop to look back. I kept going, slipping on a step at one point and nearly falling down the stairs, not wanting to see what, or who, was there.

———

PANTING HARD, I made it to the locker room. There wasn't a line anymore, but thankfully, it wasn't empty either; two of the three showers were in use, and someone was in one of the toilet stalls. My heart was still pounding and shivers raced through me as I punched in the locker code; I was glad to not be alone.

Each cubicle had a small dressing area in front of a glass shower stall. I hung my beach bag on the hook in the dressing area and decided to take a nice, long shower to try to calm myself down before seeing anyone else.

What had just happened?

Trying not to think about it so I wouldn't scare myself again, I got undressed and climbed in. After adjusting the heat, I washed and conditioned my hair, then scrubbed the chorine from my skin. The products had a lavender smell that reminded me of my mom.

You mean the mom who only cares about your sister? the voice in my head ridiculed me. *The mom who barely notices you or your problems?*

I turned the water hotter and let it run down my back until it got warm, then made it hotter again, angry, remembering.

Colette had just died. My mom was going to take me and Frankie to Portland to go shopping for funeral clothes, and I was planning to buy a copy of this book about an aspiring singer that Colette had loved but lost. Our closest bookstore didn't have the book in stock, so Portland was my best chance. I wanted to put the book in her casket so she could have it forever.

But then Mom and Frankie had ruined it.

"Are you ready to leave after breakfast?" Mom asked Frankie, serving her a second helping of scrambled eggs. "Remember, we're going shopping and then out for lunch, just us girls?"

"I don't need new clothes," Frankie said flatly.

"You don't have anything black—at least any nice clothes," Mom said, holding the spatula in midair. She had that look on her face like she was holding her breath.

"Wearing black to funerals is stupid," Frankie said, shoving half the serving of eggs in her mouth at once, chewing twice, then swallowing. "You should wear colors that the person liked. I'm doing that."

"Frankie, it's traditional to—"

"I don't care," Frankie interrupted. "I'm wearing a blue hoodie because Colette liked blue." She looked at my mom defiantly. "I'm not going to Portland."

Our mom had taken a deep breath, then said, "I'd like you to go with me and your sister and get something respectful to wear to—"

"No." Frankie got up, put her plate in the dishwasher, and left the cottage, leaving our mom staring after her.

"She's just upset about Colette," Mom said quietly,

making excuses for Frankie's behavior like usual. "Maybe she'll change her mind."

"But we're still going, right?" I asked.

She looked at me then like she'd forgotten I was there, like she'd just been talking to herself. "Oh . . . yes . . . I think so." She paused, touching her finger to her lip. "I need to talk to Charles. He's working the front desk, and I'm not sure it's right to leave Frankie alone right now."

"She won't be alone," I said. "Charles will be here."

"But he won't be able to check in with her if he's working," Mom said. "Maybe it'd be better if I stayed nearby." She paused, looking at me but more like *through* me. "You've gotten so tall, I bet I have something in my closet you can wear . . ." Her words had trailed off as she started down the hallway toward her bedroom.

I'd sat alone at the table for a long time after that, staring down at my empty plate, thinking how my mom hadn't noticed that I'd been out of eggs when she'd made more for Frankie, thinking how she never noticed anything about me at all.

The sound of a hair dryer brought me back to reality.

I turned off the water and wrung out my hair. It wasn't as long as Girl Sam's, but it was growing. I thought that maybe I'd grow it really long this year, and even put some streaks in it like Sam's; I wondered what my mom would say about that. Smirking, I turned toward the dressing area . . . and my heart leaped into my throat.

The shower had steamed up the glass door.

In the steam, I saw the message.

HELP ME

FIND BILLY

I jumped back against the wet tile wall, terrified.

Gooseflesh worked its way up my arms. Naked and held hostage by the words, blood pumping double time, I stepped forward and used my palm to quickly wipe away the message, like it'd mean it hadn't been there, then pushed so hard on the glass door that the handle hit the wall when it opened.

I was glad for the hair dryer because I sobbed in fear as I found my phone and texted Aunt Maureen to come and get me. I needed to get away from this place.

I toweled off and dressed as fast as I could, my clothes sticking to my still-damp skin, not wanting to pull up or lie flat in the right spots. My wet hair soaked the back of my T-shirt as I shoved everything I wasn't wearing into the beach bag.

The hair dryer shut off, and wiping tears from my eyes, I waited for the other person to leave, fearfully glancing over my shoulder to see if a new message had somehow appeared.

The steam was fading, the spot I'd erased still there. There was nothing new.

I rushed out of the locker room, head down, nerves electric. Wiping at my face again, I pushed through the double doors to the lobby and told the front desk worker to tell Karly I went home sick. I'd probably get in trouble for not telling her myself, but I didn't care.

Turning toward the main entrance, I ran smack into Izzy, hitting him hard. My forehead smashed into his cheekbone and made a *thunk* that didn't sound or feel good.

"Whoa, Tess, what's the rush?" he asked, touching his cheek gingerly.

"I didn't see you," I said, rubbing my forehead.

"I know," he said, wincing. "I was just looking for you . . . Want to play Ping-Pong?"

"I'm leaving," I said, adding, "I'm sick."

"Oh bummer," he said. "Maybe I'll text you later?"

All I could think of was the message.

HELP ME

FIND BILLY

"Is that okay?" Izzy asked, but I didn't answer. I wanted him to go away because everything was buzzing.

HELP ME

FIND BILLY

"I have to go," I said, starting toward the door.

"Okay, see ya," Izzy said, disappointment in his voice.

I heard it but didn't react. I barged out into the bright sunlight, me on the front steps of the rec center and Jackie and her friends behind the fence near the pool area, watching me.

I ignored them; they were nothing compared to this. Jackie was a girl who was jealous for no reason.

I was a girl who was either being haunted or going crazy.

No one could tell, because they couldn't hear my thoughts, but inside, I was screaming.

chapter 13

MY ENTIRE LIFE, drawing had calmed me—and I craved calm now.

Drawing had been something I could do well for as long as I remembered. I was quiet about it, but people noticed, like when the elementary school principal had selected my sketches to be on the cover of the yearbook three years in a row or when my science teacher had asked me if he could use my diagram of a frog as a teaching tool for all of his classes.

Back at the cabin, desperate for anything other than ripping my hands and lips to shreds, I took my sketch pad, charcoals, and a full can of bug spray to the rocker on the front porch.

Driving back from the rec center, Aunt Maureen had

asked if I wanted to talk, and when I said no, she respected that. Right now, she was inside playing a matching game at the kitchen table with Kane. Uncle Bran had taken the day off work so he and Kennedy could go fishing.

A blank page on my lap, a pencil in my right hand, I rocked, still buzzing inside, staring at the landscape. If I jumped the four feet from the porch, I could walk across the freshly mowed, prickly, brownish-green prairie grass until I ran into the hip-high, rickety wood fence. Just beyond that was the highway, then more prairie grass. Here and there, with tons of land between, gravel driveways led to houses dwarfed by their detached garages. Beyond the houses were shadowy gray-blue hills in front of white-capped mountains. Above it all, the dramatic sky.

Earlier, the day had been bright blue enough for sunbathing, but now menacing clouds moved in fast motion, climbing on top of each other, fighting for the best spot overhead.

I could tell it was already raining a few miles to the east—at least I thought that direction was east—because the space between the clouds and the grass was smudged, vertical streaks that made it so I couldn't see the hills and mountains there, the sun finding breaks in the clouds to sneak through.

I inhaled the fresh, heavy, therapeutic smell of rain on the range.

Looking down at the sketchbook in my lap, I brushed away a gnat that'd landed on the paper.

I needed to draw.

I couldn't draw.

It'd been clear from Karly's worksheet what my "special project" was meant to be. Since we hadn't been required to turn in the worksheet, I'd been honest—and all of my answers had pointed in the same direction.

Question: Who are you?

Answer: A sad girl

Question: What do you like to do?

Answer: Nothing now

Question: What's the most significant thing, happy or sad, that's happened to you in the past year?

Answer: My best friend died

Question: What form of art do you most identify with?

Answer: Drawing

Question: Who inspires you?

Answer: Colette

So, there it was: I needed to draw Colette. Except the problem was that I couldn't. I couldn't make my pencil touch the paper. I couldn't use pictures of her for inspiration. It sounds awful to say, but I didn't want to look at her.

You've hit a new low, not wanting to look at your best friend's face.

A dust devil formed in the driveway, and watching it spin, I thought I should take a video and send it to Frankie, but I didn't. Except then, like she'd been listening to my thoughts, she texted.

FRANKIE

M and AM are talking about you right now

TESS

??

😠 MOM AND AUNT MAUREEN

TALKING

ABOUT

U

How do you know?

Kai and I are stealing candy from the cottage

She doesn't know we're here

They on speaker

> What are they saying?

> AM says maybe M should make you come home

> That you're freaking out

> Being weird

> Maureen said I'm freaking out???

> No but basically

> I don't want to go home

When I typed it, I realized it was the truth. I didn't want to be anywhere without Colette, but I wanted to be here more than I wanted to be there.

> Ok

> Bye

> Wait, what else are they saying?

Frankie didn't reply; my phone screen said the message was delivered but not read. I pictured Frankie and Kai leaving the cottage and running out to the beach to eat whatever candy they'd found, Frankie giving Kai a tornado report and him telling her about a new skateboarding trick he'd learned.

I couldn't make myself draw a picture of Colette—or even look at one. And Frankie didn't seem changed by her death. I didn't understand it at all.

Were we really that different?

The huge red truck Uncle Bran had rented turned and bounced up the driveway toward me. When it got close enough, I saw Kennedy was in the passenger seat. Uncle Bran waved as they went by, around to the back of the cabin. I heard the truck stop in the spot between the cabin and the garage.

Heavy truck doors closed loudly; I heard Kennedy laugh at something her dad had said. It made me miss Charles.

The back cabin door opened and slammed shut; footsteps crunched through the gravel on the side of the house. Kennedy stepped up onto the porch and sat in the rocker next to mine. She had on ripped black denim shorts and a cold-shoulder black top, with a hideous tan vest that had tiny pockets everywhere. I thought for a second she was wearing a choker, but realized it was the tied cord of the fishing hat hanging down her back.

"I caught a twenty-inch brown trout!" my cousin said excitedly. "I used a Rabbit Strip Streamer fly, size eight. It was wicked awesome."

I looked at her blankly for a second, then said, "Congratulations?"

"Yeahthanks!" she said, the words running together like they were one.

"I didn't know fishing was . . . your thing?"

Kennedy shrugged. "Grandpa taught me last summer when you guys were out running around. It sucks he's not here this year." *Yee-ah*. Grandpa was on a cruise with a woman he'd met at his yoga class. "I'm going to text him a picture."

"Tell him hi," I said, rocking slowly, finding pictures in the clouds.

"So, what's up with you?" Kennedy asked, eyes on her phone, typing away.

"What do you mean?" I asked.

"Maureen called Brandon when we were coming off the river, and I don't know what she said, but it was obviously about you." She glanced at me with heavily lined eyes, then looked back at her device. "You keep screaming in your sleep."

"I thought that only happened once," I said.

Kennedy shrugged again in response.

"Is it because that ghost touched you in South Pass City—"

"It wasn't a ghost," I interrupted, unsure, wishing I hadn't told her about that.

"I mean, you kinda freaked out there. And you look like you're going to jump out of your skin every time we're in the car?" *Cah.*

Only when we drive under the animal crossing, I thought defensively.

"I don't know!" I snapped. "Will you stop asking me questions and just leave me alone?"

Kennedy looked at me, surprised.

"Whoa, cousin, I've never heard you get mad before." She grinned. "I think I like you more now."

I shook my head at her, saying sarcastically, "Gee, thanks." My eyes welled up with tears and quickly overflowed.

Kennedy stopped her chair from rocking and leaned forward. "Don't cry, I was just kidding," she said. "I know I don't always act like it, but I do like you. You're my cousin."

"I'm not crying because of that," I said, wiping away tears.

"Then what?" In her weird Goth-fisherwoman outfit, Kennedy did look like she cared.

"Either I'm losing my mind," I began, "or Colette is haunting me."

Kennedy opened her mouth to say something, then closed it again. She tilted her head to the side and asked, "Are you serious? Because I was just messing around about the whole ghost-touching thing." She laughed once. "I don't *actually* believe in ghosts."

"Well, I do," I said.

"Okay," Kennedy said. "And you think the ghost is Colette?"

I wiped away the tears that kept falling even though I was angrier than sad. "I don't know!" I said forcefully. "I know that sounds crazy, which is why I said it could also be that I'm losing my mind!"

Kennedy looked down at my sketchbook, which made me look down, too. I realized I'd been tearing the top page into paper crumbs, some now resting on my lap, some in piles on the wooden porch slats beneath my chair.

"She's who you've been dreaming about?" Kennedy asked, softer, probably pitying me.

Pathetic!

I said yes and continued to rip. Better the paper than my skin.

"And you think she's who touched your head?"

"I don't know, maybe?" I sighed, eyes on the paper. "We *were* in a ghost town." I looked back up at my cousin. "But today at the rec center, something else happened. I went up to the third floor, and it was really hot at first, then the temperature dropped. Like, a lot. And it felt like someone was there."

"For real?" Kennedy asked.

"Yes, and then I took a shower and there was a message in the steam on the shower door."

Kennedy's eyes widened. "What, like someone wrote in the steam?"

"Yes!" I said. "While I was in the shower!"

She twisted her lips in concentration. "You mean it appeared when the glass got all steamy?" she asked. I nodded. "But you didn't see anyone?" I told her I hadn't. Kennedy twisted one of the bracelets on her wrist, then said, "'Cause that's a known prank, right? You can do that with rubbing alcohol. You know that, right?"

"Of course," I said quickly.

Mean Me discounted it. *You are such a colossal liar. You did not know that!*

"Probably someone was pranking you or pranking someone else, and you saw it on accident," Kennedy said. "It is a wicked awesome classic prank."

"Except the message was for me," I said quietly.

"Did it say *Tess*?" Kennedy asked, starting to rock again, which made me think she was losing interest in the conversation.

"It said *Help me*," I said, pausing. "And then it said *Find Billy*."

"Like all one thing? Help me find Billy? Or help me . . . find Billy."

I thought about it. There wasn't a comma, but the statements were on two lines.

"The second one," I said, guessing.

"Who's Billy?"

"He's . . ." I sighed again. It was exhausting to try to explain to my cousin, who seemed to be growing less interested by the second. "Last year I told Colette a ghost story I'd made up about a guy named William. In the story, he was killed by his wife and his head was held on by a yellow scarf."

"Gnarly," Kennedy said before laughing.

"Colette kept telling me William went by Billy, and she said I should change his name to Billy the next time I told the story." I was in a trance, ripping paper and remembering. "But I never told the story again to anyone else."

"She's the *only* one you told? You're positive?" Kennedy asked.

"Yes," I said confidently.

"But there could be other Billys in the world," Kennedy said. "That message could be for anyone who lives around here and knows a Billy." She thought for a second. "I wonder how many Billys or Williams live here, though. It's a pretty small town. Then again, your Billy is just a made-up guy in a story. He's not *real*."

"Except . . ." My words trailed off.

Don't say it.

"Except?" Kennedy stopped rocking again.

Don't say it!

"What?" Kennedy asked.

146

Don't.

"Except there's this old man I saw in the park the second day we were here, and he did this really weird tapping thing when I went by him, and he wears a yellow scarf! In the middle of summer!"

"Okay, now that's weird," Kennedy said.

"And another thing," I said.

My cousin leaned forward again. "What is it?"

"In this picture I took at Rendezvous? Of the crowd at the street fair?" I took a breath. "He was in the background." I dropped the paper and put both hands to my mouth, whispering the last part through the holes between my fingers. "He was staring right at me."

Kennedy stood up so abruptly it made me jump, sending the rest of the paper crumbs to the ground.

"I think there's a logical explanation, and I'm going to help you find it," she proclaimed. "I'm doing this partly because I'm so over you screaming every night but mostly because I don't want all *this* for you." She waved her hand in a gesture that moved from my head to the floorboards and back again. "Besides, you've been through enough."

I looked away and sniffed, feeling a lump rise in my throat.

Kennedy grabbed my hands and yanked me up, too; my sketch pad dropped to the ground.

"There's only one way to know if the man is scary, dead

William-Billy or if he's just some freezing old man who likes to wear scarves," she said.

I guess I already knew what she was going to say next, but her words made my insides do somersaults anyway:

"We have to find him and ask."

chapter 14

I TOLD AUNT Maureen I needed a break from camp, and she didn't question my motives. For the next four days, Kennedy and I either rode bikes to town or had an adult drop us off. They didn't know it, but we were searching for the old man in the yellow scarf.

We'd start at the park by the general store, then make our way up one side of Pine and back down the other in what seemed like an infinite loop but usually only lasted two or three hours. That was all we could stand before heat or boredom got to us.

At first, I was afraid we'd find him.

By Sunday, I was mad we hadn't.

That afternoon, full of the ice cream we'd just inhaled

across the street, Kennedy and I sat on the park bench where I'd first seen the man.

"Maybe you imagined him," Kennedy said.

There's a word for seeing people who aren't there, the voice said with disdain. *It's called hallucinating.*

I didn't hallucinate! I said defensively in my head—and weakly out loud.

"I didn't say you did." Kennedy bounced her knee. "Want to play Frisbee again?"

"Not really." I watched a little girl fall off her miniature pink scooter, her dad rushing to help her up.

"Maybe he was a tourist," Kennedy said. "Maybe he doesn't even live here, and he's back home in Montana or whatever." *Whatevah.*

"Maybe," I said, defeated. My sundress blew in the breeze and tickled the back of my calf. "We should just have Uncle Bran pick us up and forget it. I'm going back to camp tomorrow."

"Don't lose hope!" Kennedy said with forced energy. "Remember that book we found that lists people's phone numbers and addresses? Which is so stalker, by the way. But we can use it to our advantage! We'll find every William, Will, or Billy in town, then go to their houses."

The internet had told us that there were more than four million people in the country with the name William, and that it was the sixth most popular name. Even though

Pinedale was a small town, there still had to be a lot of them.

"Okay, let's do that."

I stood up and started walking toward the exit of the park, Kennedy following me, knowing we weren't actually going to do that.

We'd hit a dead end.

———

THAT EVENING, WAITING for Aunt Maureen to finish cooking her famous spaghetti and meatballs, I drenched myself in bug spray and climbed up on Colette's rock, then called Frankie.

"Why do you always wake me up?" she said in greeting.

"It's five o'clock your time," I said, wondering why she'd been asleep instead of hanging out with Kai or getting ready for dinner herself.

"So?"

The day had clouded over; I'd traded my sundress for sweats. I hugged my knees and rested my chin on my right kneecap.

"Sorry," I said, because if I didn't, she might get mad. Frankie was big on hearing *sorry*, so I said it a lot—sometimes even when I didn't mean it.

"So, what's up?" Frankie said. She meant, *Why are you calling me?*

"Tell me something about home," I said. "Something normal."

"That's why you called?" Frankie said. "To hear about this boring town?"

"I miss that boring town," I admitted.

"You're weird," she said. "Wait, did you and Kennedy find the old man?" I'd told her some; Kennedy had told her more.

"No," I said, sighing. "He's nowhere to be found." The scent of prairie rain filled my nostrils, even though I couldn't feel the drops yet. "I think him being in the picture and the message in the steam were just coincidences," I told my sister. I told myself. "The old man was just an old man, and I got into a shower stall that had a message for someone else. It was probably just a prank." I sucked in as much of the delicious air as I could. "Colette is gone, and as much as we want to, we can't get her back. It's over."

"Okay," Frankie said before answering my original question. "They put up a new stoplight."

"Where?" I tried to sound interested. A new stoplight wasn't really the type of "something" I'd wanted to hear about home, but I'd take anything.

"By school," she said. "Also, Mia and Colin are shipped."

I sat up straight on the rock, my mouth open for a second before I remembered how much I didn't want a horsefly to fly in.

Mia had been the newest member of our friend group—until our friend group had broken apart at the seams. Until she'd said mean things about my sister and never apologized.

And for years, Colin had been my crush. It hadn't been like Jackie's crush on Izzy, but it'd been there.

"How do you know?" I asked, gripping the phone tightly, biting off a chunk of newly grown fingernail on my other hand.

"I saw them at the movies," Frankie said. "She was wearing hoops as big as those plastic bracelets we used to—"

"How do you know they weren't just there as friends?" I asked, eyes on the darkening clouds.

"Don't interrupt me!"

"Sorry," I said quickly. "But how do you know?"

"Friends don't kiss."

There it was.

Honestly, I wasn't mad at Colin. We'd flirted but had never been a thing. And after Colette died, I hadn't thought about him like that anymore. I don't know why, but the crush had vanished.

But Mia?

"I'm raging," I said angrily. "Where does Mia get off?"

"You still like Colin?" Frankie asked, making an exaggerated confused face.

"No, but Mia doesn't know that! As far as she knows,

she's going out with someone her good friend likes. That's against friend code."

"Except you told her you didn't want to be friends anymore," Frankie said plainly.

"I know, but . . ." Friendship stuff was sometimes hard to explain to Frankie, who tended to see things in black and white, no gray. It could be extremely frustrating.

And at the heart of everything was something I didn't want to admit. Sure, I'd been mad at Mia for what she'd said about Frankie, but I could've gotten over that if she'd apologized; I knew that Frankie would have. What had bugged me more was Mia's reaction to Colette's death.

Mia had acted *too* sad at first, then not sad at all, too soon.

What are you, the Grief Police? You judged Mia for being wrecked, even though you'd known Colette better and longer—but who are you to say how she should feel?

And you're mad at Frankie about how she's grieving, too. Who do you think you are?

You're an awful person.

I know. I know!

"Anyway, I thought you liked Girl Name," my sister interrupted my thoughts.

It stopped me in my tracks. Most of the time, I could do what my mom always said: *Pick your battles with Frankie.*

But sometimes, it really pissed me off that I had to, that I couldn't just treat her like anyone else. This was one of those times, and I lost my cool.

"Stop calling him that!" I shouted angrily.

Frankie looked surprised and a little amused. "His parents should have named him something I can remember."

"Izzy!" I shouted. "His name is Izzy! Maybe if you'd pay attention when people tell you things instead of always thinking about yourself, you'd remember them!"

Regretting I'd called in the first place, I pulled hard on the finger skin between my teeth and ripped all the way down to my first knuckle, blood instantly gushing out of the wound. It was probably the worst I'd inflicted.

Frankie was staring at me, looking so hurt I'd have cried if I wasn't so mad at her.

"Sorry I'm such a disappointment," she said quietly.

Then she hung up.

Alone on the boulder, wrapping my wound with my T-shirt to stop the bleeding, guilty, I said aloud,

"You're not."

LYING IN BED that night, listening to the buzz of Kennedy's loud music in her headphones, I thought of my second-grade teacher. At the beginning of the year, she'd instructed us to cut hearts out of construction paper. I worked so hard to make the sides of my heart match perfectly, taking much longer than the other students to do the simple task.

I'd been horrified at what happened next.

"Crumple them up," she said. "Smash them into a tiny ball."

I looked down at my perfect pink heart, not wanting to ruin it. But I wanted to follow instructions, too. I balled up my heart like the other kids, then smoothed it flat again when our teacher told us to.

"See those creases in your heart?" she asked.

"Yes," I said sadly. The heart looked ugly now.

"Those creases are like harmful words," the teacher said. "When you say harmful words to someone, the hurt they cause stays with that person—just like how the creases stay on your paper hearts, even when you smooth them out. That's why we have to be very careful with the words that we say to each other."

I got my phone from the nightstand and texted Frankie, telling her I was sorry for yelling, and that I hadn't meant that about her being selfish. I told her I loved her.

She wrote back *okay* and sent a thumbs-up.

She forwarded a meme of a cartoon turtle with heart eyes.

But I knew I'd creased her paper heart.

I wondered if she would ever know that she'd creased mine.

chapter 15

THE NEXT MORNING, the beginning of the fourth week of camp, I felt okay. I couldn't remember having any nightmares and I'd slept without waking up a bunch.

I showered and dried my hair, then pulled the sides up into a messy knot on the top of my head, the rest long and wavy. I put on mascara and tinted lip balm and a sleeveless lavender shirt that I'd always liked wearing.

I hummed along with the music Aunt Maureen chose during the drive to the library, even though it was old, guitar-heavy parent rock. Kane danced in his booster seat as best he could while being strapped down, arms and legs flapping, sometimes to the beat.

"TETH, YOU'RE PRETTY!" he shouted over the music as we were pulling into the library parking lot, warming me from the inside out. "YOU'RE EVEN ALMOST AS PRETTY AS MINNIE MOUSE, TETH! ALMOST!"

I hugged Kane before I went inside, and he hugged back, his squishy, sticky hands with dimples on the knuckles gently patting me on the back.

My mood stayed up at camp; we were learning to sculpt.

I was surprised by how much I liked it once I got started, and by how much it shut up the mean voice in my head. I'd thought I'd hate it, since sculpting was what we'd done in art class at school right after Colette died. And here, at first, when Karly turned off the lights in the room with the labyrinth floor, telling us to pay attention to the hourlong movie on the basics of sculpture, Mean Me was noisy.

There's no way you're going to be able to do this. You can barely draw.

And you're not even taking notes. Who do you think you are?

Quick! Pretend you're sick again and bail before you humiliate yourself.

But after Karly handed out lumps of gray clay and full spray bottles of water so we could keep the clay wet and told us to choose from a ton of tools on her desk to experiment with, after I started messing around with different scrapers, wire-end thingies, pokey sticks, spatulas, and texturing tools, the weight on my shoulders started to lift and the voice went away. All we had to do was create texture—

any texture. Smooshing and smoothing and shaping the clay made me think of . . . nothing.

I didn't think about how I'd hurt my sister. I didn't worry whether anyone in class was judging what I was making, whether Izzy was mad at me for not texting him back all weekend (because I hadn't known what to say), or whether Jackie was scowling at me. I didn't bite my nails (because they were covered in clay). I didn't miss home. I didn't obsess over the man in the yellow scarf.

I didn't think about Colette.

I just made texture. I used certain tools to take away pinches of clay, and different tools to add them elsewhere. I sculpted mini mountains and valleys, over and over, in a pattern that ended up looking like dragon scales. It was mesmerizing.

Way sooner than I'd thought possible, Karly called, "Time for lunch!"

Disappointed, I cleaned up my space and my hands, the worries that working with clay had pushed away rushing back into my brain like a fast tide.

Except then Izzy was there, wearing a vintage Batman shirt, smiling at me.

"Good talk this weekend," he said, shuffling his feet.

"Ohmygod, sorry I never texted you back," I said.

"Yeah," he said. "Are you feeling better?"

"I am, thanks. Seriously, though, that cat meme was funny. I just had a lot going on. And sorry about how I acted at the rec center. Sorry for being . . . short."

He looked at me with a silly expression. "Actually, I think you're pretty tall, unless you're from Themyscira."

I stared at him, confused.

"Wonder Woman's planet? No?"

"I mean sorry for—"

He cut in, laughing. "I know what you mean, I'm just kidding. It's all good. That was a lot of sorrys." He got his reusable lunch sack out of his bag. "Hey, hurry up or we'll have to sit at the picnic table with the splinters."

Relieved that Izzy wasn't mad at me, I got my sack lunch and followed him out of the room.

We ate at the good picnic table with the Sams, Jasmine, and Axl, all of them mostly talking about how hot it was and how much they wanted to go jump in Fremont Lake. This gave Izzy the idea that everyone should go on his family's pontoon boat next Saturday for his birthday. I'd never heard of a pontoon boat, but they all seemed to think it was a great idea, so I agreed to ask my aunt and uncle for permission.

"I'll get my brother to come," Izzy said. "He's sixteen." I felt like he thought I'd understand why that was significant. I must have looked confused, because he added, "You can operate a boat without an adult when you're sixteen."

"Ohhhh," I said slowly, nodding, fresh nerves breaking ground about the thought of going on any type of boat with a bunch of kids, whether one of them was sixteen or not.

I tucked in my bottom lip and bit, feeling the sting, tasting blood.

Everyone made plans for Saturday.

"You don't have to go in the water," Izzy whispered. "Lots of people don't. It's just fun being out there. And I promise my brother knows what he's doing. He acts like an adult, which is annoying but good at the lake."

Izzy and I held each other's gaze, and I had to admit that something about him made me feel calmer. Being next to him was sort of like working with clay.

"Okay, I'll ask."

⌒

"YOU SEEM HAPPY," Aunt Maureen said, glancing at me as the minivan picked up speed on our way out of town late that afternoon. I rode in the passenger seat this time, since Kane hadn't come along. He always wanted me to ride with him, and though I missed his one billion questions about every detail of camp, it was nice to be able to see the road.

"I had a good day," I admitted, trying to keep my smile under control.

"Oh, honey, that's great!" Aunt Maureen looked genuinely

happy for me, not distracted like my mom looked some-times when I tried to tell her things.

Stop hating on your mom. She works hard for you. You're so ungrateful.

I know.

"Tell me about it," Aunt Maureen said, turning off the radio altogether so she could hear me.

"Well, we're learning to sculpt," I began, before telling her about the four sculpting techniques and how Girl Sam had said that my dragon scales were the coolest texture in the class and a lot of people had agreed.

"I can't wait to see it," she said after I'd talked way too much, and I believed her.

"Thanks for listening," I said quietly, looking out the window.

Aunt Maureen put her right hand on mine, keeping her left on the wheel.

"I get it, Tess, I really do," she said. "I always felt unheard as a kid. I was the classic middle child, always feeling like your perfect mom and our clown of a younger brother were the kids my parents loved most." She paused, then added, "It's hard when the others have bigger personalities."

"It is," I said, my eyes still on the landscape. It'd rained earlier, but it was clear and sunny now, the sagebrush greener than brown: more fern than moss.

"But knowing your mom like I do, and being a mom

myself, I can tell you that we had it wrong, you and me," she said, putting her right hand back on the wheel.

"What do you mean?"

"Moms love their kids differently, but in equal amounts," she said. "I don't know if that makes sense to you, but it's true. Sometimes Kane is the easier kid to love. It doesn't mean I love him more than Kennedy. I love that girl fiercely." She paused. "Moms love their children. Your mom loves Frankie—and she loves you . . . both of you, fiercely. You'll understand someday when—"

The animal darted in front of the car without warning. It sprinted, right to left. Or right to middle, before I heard the *thunk thunk* of the van tires rolling over it at seventy miles per hour. Aunt Maureen didn't have time to swerve or stop or react at all.

We both gasped, then she checked behind us and slowed down quickly. She pulled the van onto the shoulder. "Did you see what it was?"

I shook my head, nail between my teeth, trying not to look at the lump in the road behind us in the side mirror but failing, staring at it anyway. It wasn't moving.

"I need to go make sure it's . . ." She pressed the button to make the lights flash. "Not suffering."

"Do you want me to go with you?" I asked, hoping she'd say no.

She shook her head. "Stay here. I'll be right back."

I inhaled and realized I'd been holding my breath. Three cars raced by, one right after the other, making the van shake with their momentum.

"Be careful," I told my aunt.

"I will."

After checking for more cars, Aunt Maureen jumped out of the van and started walking toward the animal, careful to stay as far away from the highway as she could. She waited on the shoulder for an RV to pass, then stepped out and hovered over the lump for a few seconds, shaking her head. I already knew it was dead. I'd had my eyes on it since we'd hit it; it hadn't moved.

Waiting for Aunt Maureen to jog back to the car, it was like my brain changed channels and I registered what was in front of me for the first time. I'd been so busy looking back, I hadn't been able to see what was right in front of me.

The wildlife crossing.

Invisible monsters breathed on my neck, whispering things I couldn't hear. Fairies danced; my stomach pulled tight.

"I think it was a rabbit," Aunt Maureen said as she got back in the driver's seat.

"You couldn't tell?" I asked, eyes on the animal bridge, watching for movement, for anything. As usual, nothing was there.

Aunt Maureen shook her head. "It was too . . ." She didn't finish her sentence. My dark brain finished it for her.

Mangled.

Unrecognizable.

"It was so close to the animal bridge," she said, glancing over her shoulder before pressing hard on the accelerator to get us up to highway speeds in a hurry. "It's too bad it didn't use it."

"Yeah," I said, holding my breath as we went under the crossing, the world blinking for just an instant. "Too bad."

chapter 16

THURSDAY, I WAS late to camp; otherwise, things would have been different.

Uncle Bran would drop me at the library on his way to the Green River; he, Kennedy, and Kane were going fishing again. I was happy to have art camp as a reason not to go myself, because the idea of hooking a fish in the face made me feel like throwing up.

But getting four people in the car on time was a struggle. Kennedy overslept, then lost her lucky fly, whatever that was, then had an argument with Aunt Maureen about what the term "proper breakfast" meant.

Then, after Uncle Bran returned to the two-row rental truck for the third time, Kane's lucky bear in hand, Kane announced that he had to go potty. I've always hated being late, so I wanted to scream; instead, I bit my tongue on purpose and stared angrily out the window, not saying anything.

Twenty minutes after camp had started, I rushed through the library stacks toward the meeting room with the labyrinth floor. I was between the kids' and mystery sections when a mom with a baby stroller set off the front-door alarm. That's why I turned. That's how I saw.

I'd stopped looking, and there he was: the old man with the yellow scarf.

He was sitting at a round table near the wall of windows, a small pile of books in front of him, staring outside instead of reading or looking curiously at the front-desk person, who was now struggling to turn off the alarm. The man looked the same, with wispy white hair, sunken cheeks, and dark circles under his eyes. He wore ecru pants and a tawny sweater—plus the yellow scarf.

Billy.

I froze, steps from the hallway that led to the meeting rooms, wishing Kennedy were there. Those days we'd looked for him, I'd been okay thinking of this moment because my cousin had been with me. I'd never expected to face him alone.

I took a step toward camp, not wanting to do it. But then

I took out my phone and casually snapped a picture. I texted it to Kennedy, moving between two stacks, biting my nails until she replied.

KENNEDY

NO FREAKING WAY! IS THAT HIM???????????????

TESS

yes

in the library

what do I do?

Ask him if he's Billy, ovbs!

So weird tho . . . like just walk up to this old man and ask if his name is Billy?

OF COURSE

THAT WAS ALWAYS THE PLAN

Do it

Tell me what happens

Kennedy's braver than you. She'd already be over there.
Frankie would, too.
But here you are, frozen like an iceberg, worthless.

Shaking my head, I checked the clock high on the wall: I was so late. Just then, the alarm went silent. My ears rang. The man didn't react to the silence either, and I wondered if he was deaf.

Only one way to find out.

I put my phone in my pocket, adjusted my backpack, and walked toward him. When I was just a few steps away, he noticed me, his cloudy gray eyes snapping suddenly to my face.

I wanted to run.

His spotty hands were on the table, like he was ready to type on an invisible keyboard. Once he saw me, with every step I took toward him, he tapped his right index finger on the table. I was desperate to flee, but I thought of Kennedy's and Frankie's braveness and pretended it was mine.

The old man stopped tapping when I stopped walking.

"Hi," I choked out before clearing my throat. "I'm Tess."

"Hello," he said, his voice higher than I thought it'd be. I hugged myself, holding my elbows, as he asked, "Is it time?"

"Um," I said, digging my fingertips into my pokey elbow bones. "It's nine thirty?"

"Is it time?" he asked again, his right hand shaking slightly.

"I don't know," I said, looking to see who was around, expecting the library to have cleared like it was the apocalypse. Instead, a mom read to her child, two high schoolers giggled near the computers, and an older woman pushed a book-filled cart. I turned back to the man. "Is your name . . . Are you Billy?"

After a long pause, he said, "William Longley." His eyes shifted to a spot over my shoulder. "Originally from Old Evergreen, Texas."

A shiver ran up my body; I dug so hard into the soft part around my elbow bones with my now-freezing hands, I sent painful shocks into my shoulders.

"Do you have something to tell me?" I made myself ask. I had to know.

"It was murder," he said, and I took a step back. He tapped his finger off the beat of my step, not expecting it.

"Who was murdered?" I asked, hunched in on myself, not wanting the answer.

You can't be talking about Colette.

Can you?

I wanted to get away from him; I took another step back. His eyes had wandered toward the window again, so he didn't tap.

"Is it time?" he asked, looking out.

"Time for what?" I whispered, afraid of the answer.

He looked at me again, sharply.

"You know," he said, annoyance in his voice. "Time for the girl to come back."

chapter 17

KARLY DIDN'T SAY anything about my tardiness when I walked in and slinked into my seat. She just came over and quietly said, "We're working on our sculptures or personal projects today. Your choice."

The room was filled with soft instrumental music, and Karly had lit a candle on her desk that smelled like the forest, but not in an overpowering way.

I flashed weak smiles back at Jasmine and Izzy, screaming on the inside about what had just happened, about talking to a man in a yellow scarf named William about murder and returning girls.

Gathering the tools for sculpture seemed too daunting. My hands shaking, I got out my sketchbook, flipping past failed attempts at portraits of Colette. I knew I couldn't draw anything real in this state, but I needed to draw *something*, I was so amped up.

Opening my pencil box, I dug for my favorite—but it wasn't there.

I looked at the floor under my table, then twisted around in my seat. I stood up to see if it was on my chair, thinking I'd left it there yesterday.

"What's wrong?" Boy Sam asked, manicured eyebrows raised. He reminded me of my dog, Pirate, always ready to spring into action. Only both of Boy Sam's eyes worked.

"I can't find my favorite pencil."

"What's it look like?" he asked, eyes on the floor. "I'll help."

"That's okay," I said. "I'll just use something else."

"But it's your favorite," Sam said, leaning closer and whispering, "I need an excuse to procrastinate anyway. Not feeling it today." He stood, too. "What type of pencil is it?"

It didn't seem like Sam was going to give up, so I gave in. "It's a 3H," I said. "The outside is silver."

"On it," he said, turning and walking the rows, checking the floor and people's desks and even the garbage, like someone might have thrown it out. After we'd searched the room, Sam stopped and folded his arms over his compact chest. "Anyone seen a silver 3H?" he said loudly. "Tess is missing hers."

I froze, right in front of Axl's desk, instantly humiliated

that now everyone was looking at me—including Jackie, who was way across the room, holding a clay cutting tool in midair.

In her royal-blue T-shirt that made her eyes stand out, short skirt, and loose braid, I knew she was pretty, but it was hard to see that through her lemon-faced expression.

"Use another pencil," she said, rolling her eyes. "You totally interrupted my flow." Louder, she added, "Karly, will you make them sit down?"

"I think we can give Tess and Sam a second," Karly said, barely looking up from what she was writing.

"This is so lame, disrupting everyone," Jackie went on, staring right at me. "First you're late, and now you're freaking out about a pencil."

"Shhh," Karly said. "Let's all calm down."

I'm not freaking out! I shouted in my head.

But no one knew how fast my heart was beating. Or that the right side of my lip felt funny, like it was falling asleep, pins and needles poking me from the inside out when I touched it.

"I know *someone* who needs to calm down," Izzy said, shooting angry eyes at Jackie. Her cheeks turned pink. Izzy said to me, "I have a 3H you can borrow, Tess."

"Problem solved!" Karly said, turning up the music. "Let's get back to work, okay?"

I felt light-headed; I just wanted to sit down.

"Thanks, Izzy," I said, taking the loaner pencil.

"Don't chew on it," he joked.

"Chewing on a pencil's better than chewing on your fingers," Jackie muttered, her eyes still on her project.

I don't think Izzy meant to do it, but he glanced down at my hand, before telling Jackie to mind her own business. I rushed back to my seat, dropping hard onto the wooden chair.

My heart felt like I'd had three Cokes at a sleepover, and as I stared at the bright white paper, my right eye got blurry. Then it got fuzzy, like I was looking through a black-and-white kaleidoscope. The right part of my lip was definitely numb now, and my right hand was tingling, too.

"You guys," I said, too quietly at first. I couldn't get a deep breath.

"You guys!" I said loudly. Everyone looked at me again; I heard Jackie groan.

"What now?" she asked.

"You look kind of . . . off," Boy Sam said quietly, concerned.

Izzy turned in his chair, his dark eyebrows knitted together. I could only see him clearly out of my left eye, but it hurt to look at him at all in the bright, sunlit room. I wanted to cover my head with a blanket.

"Karly?" Girl Sam said loudly. "Tess looks really pale. I think she needs help."

Karly came over quickly, telling the other campers to

give me some space. She put her hand on my forehead like my mom did.

"You don't have a fever," she said before telling Axl to go get me some water.

"Do you need to throw up?" Karly asked, prompting most of the kids to instinctively lean away. I shook my head. "Well, can you tell me what hurts?"

"Nothing, exactly," I said truthfully. "I just feel really weird. Like there are stars in one of my eyes. And I feel light-headed."

"I think you're dehydrated," she said. "Let's get you some water, and if that doesn't work, I'll call your aunt to come and get you." I was glad that people were starting to refocus on their work. Izzy was still watching me, though. "I'll be right back," Karly said. "I'm going to see if there's a Popsicle in the back room."

"Talk about dramatic," Jackie muttered after Karly had left, loudly enough for everyone to hear. "Way to make the day about you, Tess."

"You did *not* just say that," Girl Sam said, snapping her head to the side. "You should talk! You think the world revolves around you."

"I do not," Jackie snapped.

Girl Sam tsked. "Listen, you don't know what's going on with every other person in the world, all right? Maybe other people are going through things you know nothing about."

She pursed her lips together. "I mean her best friend *just* died. Cut her some slack."

"What?" Jasmine asked, right as Axl returned with the water. He set it on my desk while Jasmine pummeled me with questions. "Is that true? Why didn't you say anything? What happened? Are you okay?"

"I didn't really want anyone to know," I said, using my hand to shield my eyes like a visor. I wanted someone to turn off the lights.

"Oh, damn," Girl Sam said, slapping her hand over her mouth. "I'm so sorry, Tess. I forgot it was a secret."

I caught Izzy's knowing glance; he didn't say anything.

Jackie looked at Girl Sam, muttering, "Way to go."

"It's okay," I told Sam. "It was an accident." I closed my sketchbook and put it away, then stood and slung my bag over my shoulder, feeling like my head was a balloon that was going to float off into the sky. I needed to leave. "I'm going to find Karly."

"I'll go with you," Izzy said, getting up and moving toward the door. When we were almost there, he said to Jackie, "Forget the birthday cake this year, okay?" He gestured at me. "She's making it."

Even with one eye, I saw Jackie's stricken expression.

In the hall leading to the main part of the library, Izzy whispered, "I didn't mean . . . You don't need to make me a cake. It's so weird and old-school that she does that. I don't want *anyone* to make me a cake, except maybe my mom. I just wanted her to know . . ."

"I know," I said.

I felt like I was walking through a fun-house tunnel instead of a hallway.

Karly was on her way back with a Popsicle. "No better?" she asked.

"No, I need to go," I said.

"Okay, come with me," she said, adding over her shoulder, "Izzy, you can go back to the room now. Tell everyone I'll be back in ten minutes."

He waved, told me he'd text me later, and left.

Karly and I went outside so I could eat the Popsicle while we waited for Aunt Maureen, since there was no food allowed in the library. Moving through the stacks, seasick, I tried to concentrate on watching where I was going. I mostly stared at my sandals; it hurt to look up. But I did once, just to check.

William was gone.

chapter 18

IT'D ONLY BEEN a migraine, but it'd felt like dying. Thankfully, Saturday, I was better. Aunt Maureen and Uncle Bran said I could go to the lake with the others—after Aunt Maureen insisted on talking on the phone with Izzy's mom, and only if Kennedy went along. Unlike how Izzy had described his brother, I would have described Kennedy as someone who did *not* act like an adult, so I wasn't sure why they felt I'd be safer with her there. But she'd been nicer lately, so it was okay.

"Did you say your name is Sep?" Kennedy asked as she shook Izzy's brother's hand, flirt face in full effect. We were on the shifting dock, a three-story lodge behind us, the lake in blues and greens stretched out in front.

"Seb," Izzy's brother corrected Kennedy. "Short for Sebastian."

"Wicked," Kennedy said, "like the crab in *The Little Mermaid*. That crab's so fricken funny." She saw me watching her. "What? I can't like Disney movies?"

I smiled but didn't answer.

Kennedy and I were both in shorts and tank tops over our swimsuits, but her outfit was ripped and edgy and mine was basic. At least I had my hair pulled back in a messy bun, front pieces hanging down like Colette used to say looked good on me.

Cute hair doesn't cover up crazy.

Am I? Or is Colette really trying to talk to me through William?

You just answered your own question, Mean Me said. *Crazytown!*

"How's it going?" Izzy asked. He had on black swimming trunks and an olive-green T-shirt with a bear in a park ranger hat on it.

"Good," I said, forcing myself to get it together. "Happy fourteenth birthday! You *are* turning fourteen, right?"

"Thanks, yeah," he said, laughing. "I'm officially old enough to get a job." He cocked his head to the side. "How about you?"

"I'm still thirteen, but my birthday's later this mo—"

The dock shifted, and I gasped, putting my hands out to my sides to steady myself.

Izzy laughed. "Don't you live right by the ocean?"

"Yes, but I don't go sailing on it!"

"I would," he said.

I pictured us there, Izzy and me, the ever-blowing wind making his wild hair fly all over the place, him smiling with his whole face, all the way to his dark and light brown sunburst eyes.

"Izz, I get that it's your day and all, but I could use some help here," Seb said, struggling with one of the ropes that was attached to the boat.

"Got it," Izzy said, making a face that his brother didn't see before grabbing another rope.

Seb and Izzy looked alike enough to be siblings, with matching smiles, sharp noses and chins, and dorky foot-wear. But if I were to draw Seb, I'd start with umber, whereas Izzy's darker hair and eyes would be better in sepia.

"What activities are we doing today?" Jake asked, appearing in bright blue swimming trunks and a multi-colored mock-neck swim shirt, a straw hat, and huge yellow sunglasses.

"Hey, buddy," Seb said, looking over his broad shoulder. "I think the usual. Floating and swimming and hanging out. Want to grab a line?"

"Activities?" Kennedy asked me, confused. "Are we at a five-year-old's birthday party?" *Pah-dee.*

"Shhh," I said to her. "Jake likes schedules . . . like Frankie."

Kennedy nodded knowingly and didn't mention it again.

Jake, Izzy, and Seb worked together to pull the boat close, tightening the ropes around poles on the dock. Then Seb and Jake jumped aboard while Izzy, Kennedy, and I passed them grocery sacks of food, a loaded cooler, and our personal bags.

The pontoon was a floating rectangle about the size of half my bedroom at home, with a steering wheel on the right side in the middle of the boat instead of up front like I'd expect. The center part had a navy-blue canopy overhead and cushioned benches around the outside.

"I call the back!" Girl Sam yelled, shaking the whole dock as she ran down.

Boy Sam, Jasmine, and Axl sauntered behind her. A red SUV beeped twice as it backed out of the parking lot next to the lodge.

I introduced Girl Sam, Boy Sam, Jasmine, and Axl to Kennedy. Then we all boarded the boat; my heart raced as I stepped from the only-somewhat-still dock to the definitely moving floating rectangle. Once the ropes were untied and everyone was in life vests, Seb carefully maneuvered the boat out to open water, managing not to hit the other boats that were parked nearby.

I sat with Girl Sam on a bench facing backward. The boat went slow at first, then picked up speed, leaving the lodge behind. The propeller hung off the back, cutting through the water, pushing us forward, leaving a mesmerizing trail of crisscrossing waves behind us.

The farther we got from the lodge, the less I worried about William or the animal crossing or Colette. I didn't bite my nails or beat myself up. Being on the lake felt like I'd taken a gigantic chill pill.

"How big is it?" I shouted to Girl Sam, gesturing to the water. It was hard to hear over the motor.

"Ten miles?" she asked back.

"Wrong," Jake shouted, having heard us. He was facing front, on a bench back-to-back with ours. "Fremont Lake is twelve miles long and a half mile wide."

Girl Sam said, "Thanks, Jake!"

It was super windy with the boat moving so fast. Girl Sam worked her hair into a low ponytail, then put on a trucker hat with a buffalo in front of a sunset.

"I like the buffalo," I shouted.

"It's a bison, not a buffalo," Jake corrected me. *Aren't they the same thing? No, dummy!* "The bison is the state animal of Wyoming. Also, about the lake, it's six hundred ten feet deep. In the winter, there's the Big Fish Ice Derby. My grandma won it once."

The thought of walking on ice made me shiver.

"Thanks for the information," I shouted. "I guess you're the Wyoming expert around here."

"I am," he said, like this was an undisputed fact.

Jake's bench made an L shape that ran up the left side of the pontoon; Kennedy was lounging on the other part of the L, stealing glances at Seb. Just as I was thinking she was probably going to embarrass me with her flirting ways, she struck up a conversation with Jake about fishing. Jake's eyes lit up.

Happy, I refocused on the crisscrossing waves.

"Hey." Girl Sam nudged me with her shoulder. "I'm like *so* sorry for outing you in class the other day." She was talking loudly enough for me to hear, but had moved closer to my ear so probably no one else could.

"You already apologized a million times over text," I said. "Seriously, don't worry about it. It's really okay."

"I know, but I just feel bad, like maybe I caused your migraine, you know?"

I laughed, shaking my head. "My mom caused it, since I inherited them from her."

Girl Sam leaned away and raised her eyebrows high enough I could see them over her sunglasses. "Oh yeah? Your mom sucks like mine?"

"Sometimes, yeah," I admitted, immediately feeling

guilty, as if my mom could hear me right now. "But I don't mean like that," I said quickly. *Yes, you do.* "I guess she's had bad migraines all her life. She never told me."

She gives me her migraines, but not her attention.

Shut up, you ungrateful princess!

"Promise you're not mad?" Sam asked, seeming to really care. She was a nice person, someone I realized I might even want to keep in touch with when I went home.

Home felt so far away.

"I promise," I said.

Sam held up her pinkie for me to shake. Even though it ripped my heart in half, remembering the millions of pinkie promises Colette and I had made, I did it anyway.

Seb slowed the boat and killed the motor, leaving us floating in the middle of the lake. Birds chirped all around us, their songs bouncing off the steep, sharp hills that surrounded the water. The pontoon settled to a gentle rocking motion, one-inch waves lapping against the side of the boat. The lodge was miles away, and huge cauliflower clouds were both above us and reflected on the surface of the water.

I helped Sam set out snacks on top of the storage compartment where our life vests had been, and everyone loaded up plates of cheese and crackers, deli meats, cut veggies, popcorn, and birthday brownies with caramel swirls that Izzy's mom had made. Most of us sat down on the floor of the boat, up front, in a misshapen circle.

"Let's go around and say one nice thing about Izzy, since it's his birthday and all," Jasmine said, pretty in a sheer black cover-up with a white bikini underneath and a huge sun hat. She looked ready for a tropical vacation.

Everyone agreed, and Jasmine told Axl to go first. He swallowed a cracker and said, "Props to you for taking us out today, man."

Jasmine shook her head. "I meant something nicer. Like"—she looked at Izzy—"you're thoughtful. You brought me my math homework for a week when I got bronchitis last winter."

Izzy's cheeks turned pink as he went to get more food. I'd barely started eating, and his plate was empty. Since the motor was off, he could still hear us from the back of the boat.

"He loaned me his copy of *Turbo Seventeen*, since our moving boxes aren't here yet," Boy Sam said. "That was cool."

"I wondered where that went," Seb said jokingly, adding, "He's also a halfway decent brother."

Instead of coming back to the circle, Izzy kept his distance, eating his second helping standing up. He shifted from one retro sneaker to the other, obviously uncomfortable with everyone talking about him—but judging from the grin he was fighting to contain, seeming to like it, too.

"What do you like about my brother?" Seb asked Jake, who was stuffing his third brownie into his mouth.

Jake seemed to think about it for a few seconds, long enough for him to swallow the brownie. "He never laughs at me. He also never tries to touch me or my turtle and will sometimes but not always play wall ball."

Seb half smiled, and Izzy said, "Thanks, Jake."

Girl Sam's hand shot up in the air. "Remember when Izzy did magic in the fourth-grade talent show?"

"No," Jake said flatly.

"Totally," Jasmine said, laughing. Axl busted up and pointed at Izzy, who rubbed the left side of his forehead in embarrassment, covering half his face in the process.

"Who wants to go swimming?" he asked, kicking off his shoes.

Girl Sam turned so she was facing me and Boy Sam. "You know that trick where a volunteer has to pick a card, right?" We nodded. "He totally did that, but like, he couldn't get the card right. He kept trying and trying, and all the other kids were laughing, and he just kept going like . . . like . . ."

"Spider-Man," Axl said, cracking open a sparkling water and dumping half of it down his shirt when he drank it.

"What is it with you and spilling things?" Jasmine said, laughing.

"He needs a sippy cup," Girl Sam said. To Izzy, she said, "I like that you keep on trying when things don't work . . . just like Spider-Man."

Jasmine and Boy Sam said, "Aww," in unison, and Izzy's face seemed like it might explode soon, and suddenly he threw off his life vest and shirt, took two steps backward, and dove into the lake.

"I guess he's done with the game," Boy Sam joked, making everyone else laugh.

"Can't imagine why," Kennedy said sarcastically, shaking the longer side of her hair out of her face and glancing at Seb. "It was pretty lame."

Jasmine's face fell; it'd been her idea.

"It was *nice*," I said, too quietly, because everyone started talking about other things. I don't think Jasmine heard me, and I didn't know why Kennedy had been rude in the first place. I wondered if that was how she always acted around boys she thought were cute.

Axl, Jasmine, and the Sams decided to join Izzy, setting their plates aside. Kennedy stood up, too, taking off everything but her bikini, making me glad that Izzy was already in the water.

She asked Seb, "Are you coming?"

"A captain never leaves his ship," he said, patting the dashboard of the driver's station.

Kennedy shrugged and jumped into the water, screaming

when she surfaced, the sound bouncing off the hills around us. "It's fricken freezing! Thanks for the warning, jerks!"

Izzy laughed before diving under the water. When he came up, he told Jake to toss him a donut pool float. One by one, people splashed off the back of the boat except me, Jake, and Seb.

"Cribbage?" Seb asked Jake.

"Definitely," Jake replied.

They got out a narrow wooden board with a bunch of holes in it and set it up on top of the cooler. I went to the front of the boat and sat down in the space where there was a break in the railing, my bare feet dangling over the side.

His torso through the center of the rainbow sprinkle donut, Izzy paddled over.

"What's up?" He smiled brightly, his curls soaked and dripping. He looked adorable.

"Just annoyed my cousin's being . . . weird," I said.

He looked over at Kennedy as she attempted to climb on a floating raft and slipped back into the water. "She seems fine to me."

"Okay," I said, kind of wishing I was in the water, too, but then remembering that there were fish in there. I didn't want to be touched by their slimy bodies. "So, are you having a good birthday?"

"Totally." Izzy was paddling around in circles, making the sprinkle donut twirl. "I love it out here." He stopped, facing me, but I could tell he was still paddling under the water.

"Your lips are blue," I told him.

He touched his bottom lip. "Yeah, it's cold, but it's the best." He swam closer so he was only a few feet from my foot. "Are *you* having fun?"

We stared at each other for a few seconds, and it felt like something big was passing between us. Izzy started spinning again, breaking the *something*, and I thought about his question.

There I was, on a pontoon boat in the middle of a postcard with Izzy in front of me doing water ballet on an oversize donut. Behind me, Jake and Seb kept rattling off a bunch of nonsensical numbers: "Fifteen, two, fifteen, four . . ." And to my left, my cousin was arguing with Axl about someone named Big Papi.

It was strange, like one of those dreams that happen just before you wake up and seem normal until you open your eyes and realize you don't own a wombat.

Colette would have loved everything about it.

I realized I did, too.

Izzy stopped spinning and looked at me expectantly.

"So? *Are* you having fun?"

I thought of a dare Colette had tried to get me to do one time. I hadn't because I'd been too afraid thanks to a million what-if questions in my head.

You're always afraid, Mean Me chimed in. *You were born that way, and you'll always be that way.*

But . . .

I don't have to be, I thought.

One second later, I pushed off the edge of the boat, into the lake, fully clothed. When I hit the frigid water, I shrieked loudly enough to scare away a flock of birds and get the attention of everyone at the party. The life vest and the short fall kept me from going under, but water splashed into my face—shocking but refreshing.

I laughed like I hadn't since Colette was alive.

"I can't believe you did that!" Izzy said excitedly as I wiped the water out of my eyes. "Five stars!"

"Good form, Tess!" Kennedy called from her raft.

Girl Sam and Jasmine rehashed what'd just happened like sports announcers, and Boy Sam gave me a round of applause.

From the boat deck, Jake said, "I hope you brought more clothes," before turning back to his cribbage.

"You should have seen your face just now!" I told Izzy. "You looked hilarious!"

"Yeah, I did *not* see that one coming," he said. "Not from you."

"I guess I can be spontaneous sometimes," I said, beaming.

Mean Me tried to disagree, but I couldn't hear the mean

voice. Partly, it was because of the lake and its calming vibe. But mostly, it was because I heard Colette instead.

I'm proud of you, friend, I imagined her saying. *It's clear you impressed Izzy.*

I didn't do it for him, though—I did it for you.

No, I imagined her saying. *It was even better than that. You did it for yourself.*

———

ONCE I KNEW Kennedy was asleep, which meant that everyone was asleep, since Kennedy stayed up the latest, I tiptoed out of the loft and down the precarious cabin stairs to the living room. I considered going outside but didn't want to take a shower in bug spray, and besides, I was too driven. I could hardly wait to get started.

Curling my legs under me in the musty chair with the cowboy embroidery, a dim lamp with cobwebs in the shade overhead, I finally—*finally*—drew Colette. Possessed by creative focus, I lost track of time as I lightly sketched the shapes, then darkened the shadows, smudged, layered, and layered more, defining what Karly had told us were the dark and light values.

My phone sat on the wooden side table holding a picture of Colette for reference, but I hardly needed it. I could see her without looking, from her barely there eyebrows to her constantly curious expression to her confetti freckles to her snug T-shirt that said KINDNESS MATTERS to her long auburn hair, fuzzy on top with baby sprouts sticking up, loose waves spiraling from cheekbones to chest.

Completely in the zone, even though I was only drawing a portrait, I felt like I was capturing Colette's awkward strut, contagious laugh, ridiculous dance moves, beautiful voice, warmth, friendship, and heart, too.

Someone could have snuck up on me, and I wouldn't have known it . . . and they did.

"I like your picture, Teth."

I drew an unwanted slash across the right side of the page, then put my hand over my thumping heart.

"Kane, you scared me!"

He giggled. "You jumped. That was funny."

I couldn't help but laugh, too. "I guess it was," I said. "But what are you doing up?"

"I'm thirsty and also what are you doing up, too?" He tilted his head to the side; all of his hair stuck up and to the left, similar to how Frankie's friend Kai purposely tried to style his. "Will you get me some milk? Because it's too heavy for me to pick up and I could spill it okay, Teth?"

"Sure," I said, bummed about the interruption but still thinking Kane was adorable in his frog onesie with his weird way of talking.

I set down my sketchbook and charcoal and stood up.

Kane put his hand in mine for the short, seven-step walk to the refrigerator. I would definitely miss this small person.

"Maybe could I have juice please?" he asked hopefully after seeing inside the fridge.

I knew his mom wouldn't like it, but I wanted to make Kane happy. He drank the kid-size cup of apple juice quickly, making clicks each time he sucked in a mouthful. When he was finished, he handed me the cup, wiped away his juice mustache, and exhaled like he'd just run a marathon.

He wrapped his arms around my hips and hugged tight. "I love you, Teth, good night."

I hugged him back. "I love you, too, Kane."

He waved and disappeared down the dark hallway. I heard Aunt Maureen whisper for him to get back in bed when he opened the bedroom door.

The portrait of Colette wasn't finished, but it was enough for tonight. After seeing the glowing 2:46 on the microwave, I realized how exhausted I was.

Yawning, I gathered my stuff and went upstairs, gripping the handrail as I climbed. Tiptoeing across the dark loft, I heard Kennedy snoring quietly and crickets chirping loudly outside. I shivered as I went to close the open window. I pushed aside the frilly curtains and put my hands on the bottom of the pane, looking out at the dark prairie grass and the empty boulder where Colette and I had told ghost stories just one year ago. It felt like longer.

Struggling to close the sticky old window, I noticed that at the house next door, the modern cabin much larger than ours, there was a light on in a second-story window. The next moment, a silhouette appeared.

I ducked down, even though the lights were off, peering over the windowsill, watching. The silhouette stood still for as long as it takes to sing "Twinkle, Twinkle, Little Star"—I know because I could hear Aunt Maureen singing it to Kane downstairs. As quickly as it'd appeared, the silhouette vanished, then the yellow glow of the second-story light went out.

It left me with a feeling I didn't like and couldn't explain. I mean, I was awake, and Kane had gotten up. I don't know why it bothered me that a neighbor was up, too. Still, I went to bed unsettled, clutching my childhood teddy bear, hoping he would protect me like when I was a little girl.

chapter 19

I WOKE UP to find fourteen texts from my sister. She'd started sending them three hours ago, around five in the morning Wyoming time, which was four in the morning in Washington.

FRANKIE

omg

OMG

OMG OMG OMG OMG OMG

DID U SEE?

There was another 🌪 in Wyoming!!!

A bigger one! It broke a barn!

!!!!!!

It was outside a town called Meeteetse

> that town name is so cute

> Do you know if the town is cute?

> HAVE YOU BEEN TO MEETEETSE????

> TESSSSSSSSSSSSSSSSSSSSSSSSSSS!

> !!!!

> ANSWER ME

Too tired to type, no Kennedy in sight, I told my phone to call Frankie on speaker.

"Did you see?" Frankie said instead of *hello*. She didn't sound tired at all or angry that I'd yelled at her.

"I saw eight billion texts from you," I said with a yawn. "I was up really late, and—"

"Isn't it sick?" she interrupted excitedly.

"I guess," I said, not really thinking tornadoes were that sick, but not wanting to make Frankie feel bad again.

"Have you been to Meeteetse, and don't you think that town name is cute?"

She pronounced it like *Ma-teet-see*.

"No and yes," I said. "Is that how you say it?"

"Of course." She said it like she hadn't just heard of the town a few hours ago. Frankie sighed heavily. "That's disappointing you haven't been there. I want to know if it's cute."

"That's what the internet is for," I said, eyes closed. "You can learn all about Meeteetse."

"I know how to search the internet."

"I know." *Why didn't you just do that, then?* "Did you go to sleep last night?"

"You sound like Mom," Frankie said, her voice getting quieter like she was walking away from the phone.

"You sent messages in the middle of the night."

She said something I couldn't understand.

"What?"

Gobbledygook again.

"Frankie, come back to the phone. What are you doing?"

"Getting something," she said, her voice louder as she returned to wherever she'd set down her phone. I heard a loud *tink tink* noise, then her voice was *really* loud, like she'd smashed her face against the microphone. "Is this better?"

I rolled my eyes, thinking that getting Frankie to focus on a phone call was harder than trying to get a golden retriever to do math.

"The tornado was an F3 with winds up to two hundred miles per hour," Frankie said. "There's a video of a moose just hanging out next to the demolished barn. Like, 'Hi, guys, what's up? I'm a moose.'" She laughed at her joke. I heard tapping, then she said, "There are only three hundred people in Meeteetse. Talk about *teetse*." She laughed again.

"You're in a good mood."

"No, I'm not."

"Okay," I said. "Sorry, but I have to go. I have to work on my project for camp. It's the last week."

"I know when your camp ends because you wrote it on my calendar," she said in a loud, robotic monotone, breathing heavily into the mouthpiece.

"Yeah," I said. "We're going to have an art show at the end of the week." *That I'm bummed you guys are missing. If it was your show, Mom would have made it work.*

Frankie has it harder than you, Mean Me snapped. *Stop being so selfish.*

"I'm really nervous about it," I admitted, trying to connect with her. "It makes me feel like barfing to imagine everyone looking at my art."

"Everyone in the world will be at your art show?" Frankie asked, so literal.

"No," I said. "You know what I mean."

"Just don't worry about it."

I smelled bacon wafting up from downstairs. "That's easy for you to say. I worry about everything."

"I know the cure." It seriously sounded like she had the phone in her mouth.

"Can you move back from the phone?" I asked. "I can't understand you."

"No," Frankie said. "Do you want the cure for worrying?"

"Sure," I said, annoyed again, wanting to get off the phone. Wanting to have a normal conversation with my sister, for once. Wanting her to *be* normal!

Wow. Just wow.

You've hit a new level of repulsive. It's a good thing that the stuff you think isn't posted on social media for everyone to see, or you'd never have any friends, ever.

You're the worst.

The voice in my head was right: I *was* the worst. Hand over my mouth like I'd shouted it out loud, I couldn't believe I'd wished my sister to be anyone other than herself. At least I'd managed not to say it out loud.

"You have to schedule your worrying," Frankie said.

"Sorry, what?"

"You should schedule one minute every day to let yourself go wild with worrying. Other times during the day, you're not allowed to worry. You just say to yourself, 'Not until three p.m.' or whatever."

"Oh," I said, distracted by my horribleness. "That's a good idea."

"I schedule my worrying minute for one in the morning."

"When you're asleep?" I felt awful. Guilty. Like the worst sister ever.

"Exactly. I trick the system."

I smiled through tears. "Hey, Franks?"

"What."

"I love you," I said, guilt weighing on me.

"Uh-huh," Frankie replied in her close-up voice. "Cool."

I checked the clock on my phone, emotions twisted. "I'll talk to you later, okay?"

"Kai and I had Tots at the diner yesterday," Frankie said randomly. "They weren't as good as normal."

I got it, warmth spreading through me, making me homesick and guiltier at the same time. The diner was the place Frankie and I had gone when we were trying to figure out what had happened to Colette when she'd gone missing, and since then, it'd become our thing. We went every few weeks and shared Tater Tots.

I heard what Frankie was saying without saying: she missed me.

She loved me, too.

"Let's go to the diner the night I'm back," I said. "Okay?"

"Hold on," she said. It was quiet on her end for a few seconds; a calendar invitation came through for an event called Tater Tot Reunion in one week. I accepted it quickly, not believing the summer was almost over.

Frankie came back on the line and said three words before hanging up.

"See you soon."

chapter 20

IZZY SHOT UP into the air and dunked the ball on the way back down.

"I don't know much about basketball," I said, slightly out of breath, "but I think using a trampoline to dunk might be cheating."

The force of him hitting the fabric threatened to send me flying; my knees buckled as I steadied myself. I didn't want Izzy to see me lose my balance and fall into the net.

He laughed and threw the ball onto the grass. We bounced around in circles, him chasing me or me chasing him, it was hard to tell which. I'd been at his house since camp let out; Aunt Maureen had dropped us off. It was the first time I'd ever been to a boy's house, and going into the second hour, I was still so nervous I felt like I might pee my pants every time one of us bounced. Still, I loved it.

"This thing is so cool," I said. "I wish I had a trampoline in my backyard."

Bounce. Bounce. Bounce.

"Don't you have the ocean in your backyard?" he asked.

"Yeah, but it's not as fun," I said. "I mean, it's different. This is like predictable fun."

"Want to see me do a backflip?"

"As long as you don't kick me in the face."

"Don't worry, I won't," he said, moving to the center while I got as far away from him as possible. He bounced one, two, three times, then flew up high and flipped, landing steadily on his feet.

I clapped, and we resumed jumping in circles.

"Your project is cool," Izzy said. We'd done mixed media that day at camp. It hadn't been my favorite, but I'm not sure if that was because of the art style or the fact that time was running out on me understanding anything that had happened this summer.

"I like how you painted over the book page," Izzy said.

"Yours was better," I told him. "I've never seen a super-villain made from found objects before."

"It was weird." He looked embarrassed.

"It was creative!"

"That's teacherspeak for weird." He laughed. "You probably think all I think about is superheroes."

"I don't," I said, even though the thought had crossed my mind.

We were quiet for ten jumps—I counted. Then Izzy said, "I'm thirsty. I'll go get us some water."

While he was gone, I used the solo time to jump my highest yet, even doing a few quick air splits, hoping that no one could see me, wishing Colette and Frankie were here because the splits were pretty good. When I heard the back door open again, I stopped pretending to be a cheerleader, and by the time Izzy got back to the trampoline, I'd sat down.

He crawled across the surface, rolled me a water bottle, and flopped onto his back. "I'm sweaty."

"Me too."

"Sweet air splits."

"You saw that?" My cheeks burned.

"Yeah," he said with a laugh.

I lay back on the trampoline and looked up at the clouds.

"Um, so," Izzy began, not looking at me either. "I don't always think about superheroes, you know. I don't even like them that much. I mean I like them, but not . . ." He took a deep breath. "I'm saying I think about other things . . . like sometimes you."

"Oh," I said quickly, eyes wide, surprised by the confession. Was this what boys did when you went to their houses? I so desperately wanted to text Colette and ask her because she'd been to a boy's house before.

Say something! the voice in my head shouted at me.

"Do you believe in ghosts?" I asked.

Why would you ask him that?

"I . . . uh . . . no?" Izzy asked back. "Maybe? I don't know. Why?"

Well, now what are you going to do?

"Oh, no reason," I said, my face turning red. "It's dumb. Never mind."

"No really, why?" he asked genuinely.

Don't say it. DO NOT SAY IT!

"I sort of kind of think maybe I've had some ghost experiences this summer."

Ohmygod, you said it.

Izzy was horrifyingly quiet, so I quickly added, "I'm totally kidding."

"Too bad. I was thinking that was cool," he said.

"It wasn't cool—it was scary!" I shouted, making him laugh.

"Oh, you were kidding, huh? Doesn't sound like it." He nudged me with his knee and said, "You can tell me. I'm not going to judge you or anything."

And I guess that was all it took, because I told him everything, from being freaked out every time I went under the animal overpass to the ghost touch in South Pass City to feeling like I was being watched at the water fountain and the steam message at the aquatic center to the creepy old man who matched my ghost story and tapped when I was near him and told me a girl was coming back—a girl I thought maybe was my dead best friend.

"Did you just tell me that stuff so you wouldn't have to say anything about me saying I like you?" Izzy asked, still as a corpse next to me, face toward the sky.

I was disappointed he hadn't said anything about my scary experiences, but maybe he hadn't known *what* to say. What would I have said if he'd told me he thought he was being haunted?

"I guess?" I didn't move either.

"Is it because you don't feel the same or because you're embarrassed?"

I didn't have to think about it. "The second one."

I heard him exhale. "Okay, good." He waited a couple seconds, then asked, "What does the old man look like?"

I bit the edge of my fingernail and pulled, talking around it, describing the man to Izzy. "And he wears a yellow scarf, just like the man in the ghost story I told Colette last year."

"You mean a *gold* scarf?" Izzy asked, rolling onto his side, seemingly okay to look at me now. He propped his head in his palm.

"I'd call it more of a mustard, but some people might think it's gold, why?"

He pushed himself up. "Come on, I want to show you something."

My legs felt wobbly after jumping as I followed Izzy across the lawn to his house. We went in, and no one was around: not his mom, who I'd met earlier, or Seb, who'd been watching TV when we'd gotten here.

Izzy led me through the living room toward a door I assumed was the garage, but when he opened it, I saw that it was a stairway leading down to a basement. We don't have basements in Long Beach, so it felt weird following him down the plush carpeted stairs to a room *under* the house. This one was a rec room—a chilly one covered in brown and gold everything. I looked at the pennants and framed jerseys on the wall, the alternating brown and yellow pillows on the beige couch, the bright gold throw blanket tossed over one side.

"What is all this?" I asked.

"Cowboy pride," he said, pumping his fist in the air.

"I assume the Cowboys are a sports team?"

"The best sports team: the University of Wyoming. Go, Pokes!"

"Um . . ."

"Hey, we don't have any pro sports here," he said. "The

college teams are all we've got. Anyway, was the scarf brown and gold, like this stuff?"

"Just gold," I said, frowning. "But about the same shade."

Izzy scratched his head. "I'm not sure, but the man you're describing sounds a lot like my friend Casey's great-grandpa. He's like a hundred years old, and he wears scarves all the time, even in the summer, because he's hella old and freezing all the time. Casey said his house was like a sauna. He lives at a nursing home now."

"He's not really a hundred, though, right?" I asked.

"No really, he is!"

My heart was pounding. "Your friend's great-grandpa's name is William? William Longley?"

Izzy shrugged. "He just calls him his great-grandpa. Want me to ask?"

"Yes," I said, walking over and sitting down on the cushy sectional without asking, digging both pointer fingers into the cuticles surrounding my thumbs.

Izzy got out his phone. While he texted with Casey, muttering half phrases I didn't understand, I noticed not everything on the walls was full of college spirit. The wall behind where I'd been standing had nothing but framed art by Izzy; he'd signed each piece. There were paintings of mountains, a wolf, Izzy's mom, flowers, and Izzy himself. It was the best self-portrait I'd ever seen.

Since he was seemingly good at everything, I hadn't realized Izzy's preferred art style was painting.

"Nothing to see here," he said, noticing me looking at his work, waving his hands, his cell still in one. "Besides, I got the deets."

He came and sat next to me, not too close, but not like he was allergic either. I gave myself a hangnail, then pulled at it, stinging pain shooting through my thumb every time.

"His name's Richard Allen," Izzy said. "So, like . . . not William Langley."

"Longley."

"Whatever," he said, smiling.

I sighed, deflated, realizing how badly I'd wanted the man to be Casey's great-grandpa—how badly I wanted answers.

"No, but wait," Izzy said. "Hear me out." He raised his eyebrows like he was asking if I was listening; I gestured for him to keep going. "Casey's great-grandpa is a killer dude and all, but he has dementia and Parkinson's disease, so he kinda doesn't know what he's talking about."

"I'm sure he knows his own name," I said. "The old man I met said his name was William Longley."

"Weeeelllll," Izzy said, "that's the thing. Casey says his great-grandpa tends to agree with everything people say because he doesn't remember what's right."

"But—"

"I just searched that name." Izzy twisted his lips to the side. "Do you want to search or should I just tell you?"

"Tell."

"William Longley was a famous gunslinger who died in like the eighteen hundreds or something." He scratched his face. "Casey says his great-grandpa is obsessed with gunslingers. And the Cowboys." He paused for a few seconds, then added, "Also, Casey says he shakes because of the Parkinson's, so he taps his feet or hands a lot to control them or whatever."

"I'm so stupid," I said, heat creeping its way up my neck. I covered my face in my hands. "Did you ask what it meant when he asked when the girl was coming back?" My voice was muffled, but Izzy understood me.

"Just a sec." I heard him typing, then he said, "Casey says he probably meant his home health aide, whatever that is. Casey says his GG's kind of sexist and calls her honey all the time. I guess she takes him places and drops him off, like the library or park or whatever, and he's always mad, saying 'that girl' left him there for too long."

I grabbed a nearby pillow and slammed it into my face, shouting, "OHMYGOD" into it. Feeling *so* dumb for spending my entire summer freaking out about a poor man who has dementia—and *so* embarrassed to be discovering this in front of Izzy.

"I have to go home," I said, my words muffled.

I felt tugging at the corner of the pillow. "Want me to show you a failed magic trick? Or I could sing? That's pretty embarrassing, too."

"You'd probably just be good at it," I mumbled. "You're good at everything. Nothing you do is embarrassing."

Izzy laughed loudly and tugged gently at the corner of the pillow again. "I still dress up for Halloween every year."

"That's because Halloween is the best holiday of the year." It was hot under the pillow—and inside my skin.

"I use my mom's hydrating sheet masks sometimes."

I couldn't help it; I smiled picturing Izzy and his mom having a "spa day" together.

"Oh! And in sixth grade, I got a C minus in PE!"

I dropped the pillow into my lap and looked at him seriously. "That's impossible. You're lying. Who gets a C minus in PE?"

"Someone who can't square dance?" I held back laughter while he kept talking. "Why do they teach square dancing, anyway? Don't bother teaching us self-defense or CPR or something we might use in the real world. Teach us how to square dance! That'll come in handy in all sorts of practical life situations! Having a tough day? Square dance! See someone choking at a restaurant? Square dance! Find yourself surrounded by supervillains?"

"Square dance!" we said in unison, both of us cracking

up, his laugh making me laugh harder until my sides ached and tears sprung out of my eyes.

"Thanks, Izzy," I said when I'd calmed down.

"Sure, yeah, no problem," he said, looking at his feet, then back at me.

Our eyes locked, and there was a second when I thought I was about to have my first kiss. But then the door at the top of the stairs opened and Izzy's mom called down, asking if I was staying for dinner. I couldn't because Aunt Maureen was making burgers at my request, and besides, I was ready to go. It'd been a roller-coaster few hours, and I needed time by myself.

Izzy walked me to the door, but before I left, he said, quietly so none of his nearby family would hear, "I thought of one other embarrassing thing about me."

"What?" I asked so quietly it was basically a whisper.

He stepped closer, like he was telling me a secret. "I told a girl I like her on a trampoline."

My insides squished together: a softer type of nervousness. "That's not embarrassing if she likes you back."

"I don't know if she does," he whispered. Aunt Maureen honked from the driveway.

"She does," I whispered. "So I think you're good."

"Phew." Izzy looked like I'd just given him a really great present. It made me feel like I'd gotten one, too.

Tomorrow was Wednesday; there were only two days left of camp and then the art show and it would be over.

I didn't want to leave his house. We'd only just . . . I don't know. But I had to—Aunt Maureen honked again.

I stepped down to the porch and looked back, smiling up at him, smiling for real *because* of him.

"See you tomorrow."

chapter 21

I SAT ON Colette's boulder cross-legged with my sketchbook on my lap, adding finishing touches to her charcoal drawing. I'd worked on it throughout the day at camp, despite spending a lot of time staring at and daydreaming about Izzy. Even without my last-minute marks and smudges, I thought that the portrait was the best thing I'd ever made in my life.

Better than that, it was her.

I inhaled the smell of prairie grass and bug spray and smoke from somewhere in the distance, feeling something that resembled happy, though that was a hard emotion to even think about experiencing after Colette. But it was there, undeniably, and while I drew, my inner voice was quiet.

I was adding texture to the background when a shiny

black truck I didn't recognize turned toward the cabin and bounced up the gravel driveway. I made out Kennedy in the passenger seat, arm half full of bracelets dangling carelessly out the window, but the sun reflected off the windshield, obscuring the driver at first. That's until the truck pulled around the cabin and parked, facing the boulder, between the back door and the shed. Then I could see him perfectly.

Seb.

Right in front of me, Kennedy leaned across the truck and grabbed the back of Seb's head, pulling him toward her. They kissed like long-lost lovers in a movie, not even caring that I was right here! Kennedy patted Seb on the cheek, then slid out of the truck. Seb waved to me and backed away; I was too stunned to wave back.

Kennedy watched him go with her hand shielding the sun from her eyes, then turned toward me. She had on a tight black tank top with a choker, cutoffs, and white high-tops with graffiti sharpied all over them.

"Whatup, kid?" she said, beaming. "How hot is that one, am I right?"

"What are you *doing*?" I shouted, suddenly angry but I didn't know why.

"What do you mean, what am I doing?" she asked. "I'm standing here basking in the glow of that hot Greek man."

"But . . . but . . . he's two years older than you! And you barely talked at the lake!"

She smirked. "Talking's overrated. And he's only a year older than me." She gestured between the two of us. "You and me are a year and a half apart! Are you saying *we* can't hang out?"

"That's different," I said. "We're related. And we're . . . That's not what I meant." I was flustered. "Does your mom know who you were with?"

Kennedy laughed at me, holding up her palms. "Calm down, cousin, Maureen knows. She even met him. Is that better?" *Bettah?*

No, it's not! I screamed in my head. I still couldn't figure out why I was so bothered by Kennedy and Seb, but all I knew was that I didn't want them kissing like a CW show, and especially not in front of me.

You're mad because you wish you were like her, but you know you never could be.

"No, I don't!" I shouted out loud.

Kennedy looked at me funny. "You don't what?"

"Nothing," I said, shaking my head.

"You seem weird," she said. "Is this about that old man again? Because we can totally go stake him out if you wa—"

"No!" I interrupted, annoyed. "I figured out who he is, and he's just an old man who has dementia. He has nothing to do with Colette."

"Are you sure?" she asked, smiling at me. "Because it was kinda fun investigating with y—"

"I'm sure," I interrupted.

Kennedy smiled slyly. "Not even if we made it a double date with the brothers?"

I slammed shut my sketchbook and slid off the boulder, putting my hand on my hip. I didn't know who I was right now, but I wasn't quiet, polite Tess. I was angry Tess.

"Listen to me," I said, narrowing my gaze at my cousin. "We're not doing that—*especially* not with Izzy and Seb. But we're never looking for the man again, anyway. I told you I found out who he is, so just drop it. It's over!"

She looked hurt at first, then her face hardened, morphing back into the Kennedy I'd seen when we first got to Pinedale. It was amazing how quickly she could go from looking like a friend to looking like some angry girl on a punk-rock album cover.

"Whatever you say." She started walking away from me, around the side of the cabin. "I can't wait to go back to Boston. I'm sick of babysitting."

She didn't come to bed that night until so late that I should have been asleep; I pretended that I was. I didn't know what to say to her, or how to explain how I felt. All I knew was that I was upset, and that if I had another nightmare and cried out in the night, I didn't think Kennedy would rush to help me anymore.

chapter 22

THERE WAS NO art camp on Friday because Karly and several volunteers were turning the room with the labyrinth floor into a makeshift gallery for tonight. The week had happened too fast, and in just thirty hours, I'd be boarding a plane to go back home.

Aunt Maureen and I went to Jackson to shop for something for me to wear to the event. I spent most of the drive there and back texting Izzy about the best horror movie soundtracks and how weird it was that Kennedy and Seb were together. We also talked around the big issue of me leaving, typing things like:

Next week will be so weird.

I'm going to miss art camp.

The summer's gone by too fast.

I can't believe I'll miss your birthday.

I wish . . .

When we were shopping, though, I put my phone away.

"Try this," Aunt Maureen said, tossing a red floral sundress over the door of the changing room at a boutique nicer than anything there was in Pinedale or back at home. Jackson was fancy, but in a way made to look rustic, I guess. "You look lovely in red."

"Thank you," I said, trying it on. It fit me exactly right and the fabric was soft as a kitten. I opened the door and Aunt Maureen gasped.

"That's the one!" she said.

I checked the price tag and gasped myself. "It's too expensive," I whispered.

"My treat," Aunt Maureen said. "I've loved spending the summer with you, and I'm so proud of you for all your hard work at camp." She reached out and squeezed my hand. "I know it's been hard, but you're doing so well. You deserve to wear something as beautiful as you are. I mean you're beautiful on the outside, of course, but more importantly, on the inside."

You've got her fooled, Mean Me scoffed. But I didn't listen.

I turned and looked at myself in the three-sided mirror. She was right: it was the best dress I'd tried. And even though my unwashed hair was piled on top of my head and

I didn't have on any makeup, I still looked like the best me in it.

"I think I need to talk to my mom," I said, glancing at Aunt Maureen in the mirror. "I think I need to tell her . . ." I sighed. "I don't know, but something. I'll figure it out."

Aunt Maureen came up behind me, turned me around, and gave me a long hug. She took a step back.

"You know I love you, right?" she asked.

I nodded.

"Your mom does, too. And she knows you two need to talk," she said. "Everything is going to be okay, I promise."

We bought the dress and sugary coffee drinks next door and took selfies under a massive arch of antlers at the entrance to a park.

"This is so random," I said, looking at the pictures. "Colette would love it."

"That's the first time I've heard you bring her up all summer," Aunt Maureen said, surprising me. I felt like I talked about Colette all the time—but maybe that was only in my head. "It's nice."

"It's nice to me, too," I said, and while we walked back to the minivan, I told her the story about the time I hid a cardboard cutout of Darth Vader outside of the bathroom door while Colette was in the shower. Both of us laughed, remembering my best friend.

NO ONE WAS home when we got to the cabin. There was enough time for me to shower before the art show, but barely. I hurried to the bathroom with my brand-new dress, excited to wear it.

Excited to show Izzy.

I washed my hair and body under the showerhead that made the water feel like pinpricks, not using too much shampoo or soap, or it'd never rinse out. I turned the water hotter and inhaled the minty steam, feeling refreshed, wondering what Izzy would be wearing and how he'd act and if he'd like my portrait. I hadn't shown him yet.

Finished, I turned off the water and wrung out my hair, then reached out for the towel and dried off in the warm stall. With the towel on my head, I threw back the curtain and stepped onto the braided rug there to save my feet from the unheated tile.

Looking up, my heart leaped at the message on the fogged-over medicine cabinet mirror, and this time, it was *clearly* meant for me.

IT'S NOT OVER, TESS

I yanked the towel from my head and threw it around my body, then ran out of the bathroom screaming, tears streaming down my face. Uncle Bran and Kane were just getting home; Kane had been at a day camp while Uncle

Bran worked. Aunt Maureen was washing her hands at the sink. All three of them looked at me with surprise.

"What's the matter?" Aunt Maureen said, hurrying over, her hands dripping, putting an arm around my shoulders.

"There's a message in the mirror," I sobbed. "It's terrifying!"

Kane stuck his finger in his mouth and said, "Mommy." She went over and picked him up.

Uncle Bran went to bathroom to check it out. He was back quickly. "Who wrote that?"

"I don't know!" I cried.

Was it Colette, after all?

It had to be!

Who else would . . .

Just then, Kennedy came through the back door, and the memory of our conversation the day before slammed into the front of my brain. I'd yelled at her, *It's over!* The message said it wasn't.

"Was someone screaming?" Kennedy asked. "I heard—"

"YOU!" I shouted, pointing at her. "You did it!"

Aunt Maureen sighed and said, "Kennedy, did you write a message on the bathroom mirror to scare your cousin?"

"What are you talking about?" Kennedy asked. "I've been with Seb all afternoon."

"*Out* with Seb?" her dad asked, narrowing his eyes at her. "Or *here* with Seb?"

"Out!" Kennedy said, crossing her arms over her chest defensively. Her neck was red like she was allergic to something.

"Don't lie, Ken," Uncle Bran said. "You know we'll take your phone if you lie to us."

Kennedy looked at me, fire in her eyes. "If you cost me my phone because you accused me of something I didn't do and they believe you just because you're a goody-goody—"

"Leave her alone," Aunt Maureen snapped. "When you have a track record like yours, it's easy for us to think you might have done something like this."

"That's bull—"

"Hey!" both of Kennedy's parents yelled in unison.

"I'm not going to your stupid art show!" Kennedy shouted at me, her fists clenched so tightly her knuckles were turning white.

"Good!" I shouted back at her, not caring, convinced she'd written the message.

Did you write the first one, too?

If so, why?

"You're going to the art show," Uncle Bran said, cutting off Kennedy when she started to protest. "I don't want to hear it. You're going, or you'll hand over your phone."

Kennedy turned and stormed upstairs so fast that I worried she'd fall. I heard a sob let loose when she reached the loft, which made me feel for her until I thought back to our conversation again. It was just too perfect: scripted even.

It's over!

IT'S NOT OVER, TESS

I knew Kennedy did it.

Or Colette?

Both were hard to believe.

"Tess, we're running out of time," Aunt Maureen said, still holding Kane like a baby despite the fact that his feet went down to her knees. "Go get ready in our room. There's a mirror in there."

She got my clothes, toiletries, and makeup so I didn't have to go back in the bathroom, even though Uncle Bran said he'd erased the message. I didn't have time to do the hairstyle I'd wanted; I pulled half of it up in a side barrette instead.

"Ready," I said, stepping out of the room, not looking toward the bathroom.

Aunt Maureen and Uncle Bran changed like lightning. We all hurried to the car, Kennedy included—in ripped jeans and a T-shirt that said NO. No one spoke, even Kane, but he looked at me every once in a while and smiled.

I wasn't even paying attention when we went under the animal bridge, but something in me sensed it anyway, because the fairies did cartwheels on my spine. My bare arms grew gooseflesh, and I turned back, once again, hoping to see *anything*—even if it was scary. Wanting to know why that stupid bridge creeped me out every single time we went under it.

But as usual, nothing was there.

Nothing that I could see, anyway.

chapter 23

THE ROOM WITH the labyrinth floor looked magical.

It distracted me from thinking about the message in the bathroom or my anger at my cousin for probably putting it there.

Overhead, the main lights were dim, and string lights snaked around the chunky wooden rafters, twinkling brightly. There were small, high tables with crisp black linens and glowing candle centerpieces, and a food and beverage station on the far back wall.

Along the sides of the long room, each camper had a station with a table dressed in black, our names printed in glittery black calligraphy on paper tents. The tables and the walls behind them featured our individual pieces of artwork from the summer—anything that we'd wanted to turn in, including our special projects. Classical music played softly, and I guessed the candles were scented, because the room smelled like a mixture of nature and birthdays and spiced tea.

It wasn't like any gallery I'd seen, but maybe it was better.

We were ten minutes late, so it was crowded when we got there. Kennedy angrily grabbed a name tag and was quickly swallowed into the room. I was relieved to see her go so I didn't have to be on defense.

I picked up a marker from the table near the door to write my name on a sticky tag, my back to the crowd. That's when I heard a familiar voice behind me.

Very familiar.

"The line at the drink table is getting long. Hurry up!"

Gasping, I spun around to find my sister standing in front of me, wearing a maroon skater dress and slip-on checkerboard sneakers, a massive grin on her face, her normally messy hair now shoulder length and wavy cute.

I dropped the marker and grabbed her, hugging tightly. She didn't hug back, because she never does, but she let me squeeze her without protesting. I even felt her smiling against my cheek as she mumbled, "We tricked you."

I pulled away and saw my mom; I was crying before I made it the few steps to hug her, too. I'd gotten even taller, so I had to hunch, but being in her arms was still the best place ever.

"Tessy Bear," Mom said softly, rubbing my back. "We missed you *so* much!"

"I didn't think you were coming!" I said, crying with my face pressed against her shoulder.

"Maureen and I thought you'd like the surprise," she said before pulling back and wiping my tears with her thumbs. "But maybe we should have told you. Oh, don't ruin your pretty makeup! Was it a bad surprise?"

"No!" I said. "It's a good one! I'm so happy!"

My mom put her hand on her heart, smiling. "Thank goodness." She stepped back and looked me over. "My girl, you look *beautiful*. And so grown-up. That dress!"

"I can't believe you came," I said, wiping my eyes again, thinking she looked beautiful, too. She had on slim black pants and a short-sleeved black-and-white wrap top I'd never seen. Her dark hair was down, sleek and shiny.

"We wouldn't miss it for the world." She leaned in, holding my gaze; she even had on eyeliner. "*I* wouldn't miss it, Tess. Do you know that?"

I do now.

"Yes," I said, the word getting stuck in my throat. I needed to change the subject, or I'd cry more. "Where's Charles?" I asked, looking around.

"Someone had to take care of the inn," Mom said sadly, adding, "He wishes he were here."

"I just sent him seven pictures of you guys hugging,"

Frankie said next to us, eyes on her phone, typing like she was in a texting contest. "He said he feels like he's here."

"Frankie, leave him alone. He has to work," Mom said.

"I *am*," Frankie said, still texting him.

"Put the phone away," Mom said sternly, and Frankie rolled her eyes in a way only she can, and I felt like I might burst it was so good to see them again.

"Can we get a drink already?" Frankie asked, and my mom agreed, looping her arm through mine.

"Yes, and then we're going to Tess's station so we can see what she's been up to this summer."

"I know what she's been up to this summer," Frankie said sarcastically. "Where's the g—"

"Shh," I said, and she didn't even snap at me for shushing her.

We started through the crowd, my mom looking back at her sister, saying, "We actually did it! We surprised her!"

"It's a miracle!" Aunt Maureen replied. Until then, I hadn't realized how similar their voices were. It was sweet.

Everyone got a cup of punch, and we moved to the corner of the room, hovering near one of the high tables. Kane, in his shorts and button-down mini-man shirt, stared at Frankie.

"What?" she asked.

He blinked.

"Stop staring at me," she said flatly.

He blinked again, then stepped behind his dad's leg. Uncle Bran was in mid-conversation with my mom and Aunt Maureen, and didn't stop talking, telling them he wished he could work from Wyoming year-round, but he automatically put his hand protectively on Kane's back. I really missed Charles. He was the only father figure I'd ever had, and I was sad he was missing the night.

Still, I couldn't have been happier that Frankie and my mom were here.

There was a stage set up on the wall opposite us; Karly stepped up and stood behind a microphone. She had on a jumpsuit and heels, and looked different from her usual bohemian vibe—more professional.

"That's my teacher," I whispered to Frankie as Karly started talking, thanking everyone for coming and telling the parents and grandparents about all the different art styles we'd worked on this summer. Frankie pulled away from me and rubbed her ear, giving me a look. She didn't like the feel of whispers. "Sorry."

"Where's the guy?" she asked in a voice that *wasn't* a whisper.

"Ohmygod, shh," I said, my cheeks getting hot. "Let's just listen."

Frankie got out her phone and started messing around,

and I couldn't say anything because I wasn't listening either: I was staring at Izzy's back. I knew right where he was, in his gray-and-white button-down shirt and darker gray slacks with black dress-up shoes.

When Karly finished, it was as if Izzy had known exactly where I was, too, because he turned right toward me and smiled.

Frankie tracked my gaze, then drew out the longest, loudest "oooooooh" in the world. Several people nearby turned around. I wanted to kick her. "There he is."

"You don't know that."

"Yes, I do. Your googly eyes are a dead giveaway."

I turned my face toward her as Izzy made his way over. "Quick, do I have mascara under my eyes?" I asked, wiping them whether I did or didn't.

"I don't think so?"

I shook my head at my sister—the only person I knew who could answer an easy yes-or-no question with a noncommittal "I don't think so?"—and hoped for the best, because there he was, right in front of us, stuffing his hands into his pockets and looking pretty googly himself. I tried to keep my smile in check and my voice normal.

"Hi," I said in an abnormally high voice.

"Hi," he said, sounding weird, too.

I cleared my throat and hooked my thumb to the right. "This is my twin sister, Frankie."

"Nice to meet you," he said. "I'm Izzy."

"Oh, I know," Frankie said, wiggling her eyebrows. "I heard you have a trampoline and wear socks with pizzas on them."

"Oh god," I muttered. "Please no."

"I do have a tramp and sweet pizza socks," Izzy said, "but I don't have either with me right now."

"That's disappointing." Frankie frowned at him.

"These are kind of cool, too, don't you think?" Izzy said, lifting his pant leg to show her his socks with sharks.

Frankie shrugged. "Meh. Also, you're not *that* tall. And why do you have a girl's name?"

"Frankie!" I said, exasperated. Izzy was laughing at the interrogation.

"Let's go see Tessy's art!" Mom said excitedly, rescuing me.

"Good idea!" I said, wanting to get Izzy away from Frankie in a hurry.

Everyone started walking, and Izzy scooted closer, saying quietly, "Yeah, let's go see *Tessy's* art."

I smacked myself in the face. "My family is humiliating."

Izzy laughed. "All families are humiliating. At least you have a normal amount of family here. My mom invited my entire extended family and all our neighbors, too. I think there are like twenty of them! I don't even know some of the people."

"No wonder the room's so crowded!" I said.

"Yeah, but did you see Girl Sam's entourage? She wins!" He glanced down at my dress and lowered his voice more. "You look really nice."

"So do you," I whispered. "I've never seen you in pants."

He laughed silently. "I own some."

"I see that."

"Well, I'm gonna . . ." He waved in the general direction of where he'd come from. "I'll be back."

My face hurt from holding in a humongous smile. "Okay, see you."

"I like him," Frankie said after Izzy had walked away, her eyes on her phone screen.

"Good, but no more embarrassing comments when he comes back, okay?" I said.

She shrugged, committing to nothing.

"Aren't you going behind your table like the lady said?" my sister asked, the flashing screen making her face turn blue, then green, then blue again.

"Are we supposed to . . . ?" I looked around the room and saw Jasmine, Boy Sam, Axl, and the others standing between their tables and the walls.

"Yeah, weren't you paying attention? The lady said you're supposed to stay at your stations for a half hour, and all the people are going to walk around and look at your art and ask you questions or whatever. Then, one at a time, you walk around and look at everyone else's. Geez." She rolled her eyes like telling me all that had been painful.

"You were playing video games that whole time," I said. "Are you sure?"

In one movement, Frankie folded her shoulders forward and looked up at the ceiling, her chin jutting out. "How many times do I have to tell you I can do a bunch of things at once," she said flatly, making brief eye contact. "I'm getting more punch."

"Are you going to look at my—"

"Already did," she said over her shoulder, walking away. "I like the dragon scales and the picture of Colette. It's the best thing you've ever drawn."

"Wow . . . thank you," I said softly, my hand on my full heart, but she was already too far away to hear me.

The next half hour happened just like Frankie had said, with nice parents and older people asking me how I created my collage, or what inspired me to make my mixed media piece, the teenagers who'd been forced to attend lurking in the middle of the room. Kennedy was there, chatting with a group I didn't know. It was hard not to notice that Seb was moving through the stations, talking to campers about their art. Doing what he was supposed to be doing.

Why couldn't she?

Frankie appeared next to me, a half-eaten donut in one hand. "That kid is weird."

"What kid?" I asked. "Do you mean Kane?"

She shook her head, pointing at Jake. "That kid," she said. "We talked for like an hour about space and tornadoes." It'd been nowhere near an hour. "He smells like cheese."

"He's nice," I said defensively.

"I didn't say he wasn't," she said. "I said he's weird. I'm weird. You're weird. We're all weird." She took a bite of donut and gestured toward Jackie. "Except that girl: she sucks. She ignored my questions about her splatter painting. Also, I know her."

"What do you mean, you know her?" I asked, wanting to tell Frankie that Jackie was the mean girl I'd told her about, but not wanting her to say anything about it loudly for others to hear and embarrass me.

Frankie shrugged. "I just do. I've seen her."

"Where?" I asked in disbelief. "On the camp blog?" Sometimes Karly put pictures of us there.

My sister shrugged again, her eyes narrowed, staring. I was glad Jackie didn't look over, or she'd know we were talking about her.

Jackie hadn't looked at me all night, at least not that I'd noticed. Maybe she was over her jealousy, but it seemed like she'd been avoiding me.

"I don't think so," Frankie said about the blog, before stuffing the rest of the donut in her mouth. Mumbling, she added, "I'll remember eventually."

Frankie stayed at my station when it was my turn to go around and see everyone's work. Girl Sam had made a super-realistic sculpture apple, Jake's picture of the night sky was impressive, and though I didn't stop to get a close look, I thought Jackie's abstract painting seemed interesting and complex.

I did stop in front of Izzy's work when, thankfully, he was alone, because his special project was extra special— but embarrassing, too.

The painting was of a girl with straight dark hair, a long neck, dark eyes, a sharp nose, and a few faint freckles. Her expression made me feel sad and expectant and curious and nervous all at the same time. It felt just like when he'd done the manga drawing of me.

Next to the picture was a plaque that said:

GIRL WITH SECRETS
By Isaakios Kosta

"I don't have secrets," I said, ducking my chin.

Izzy shrugged. "I wanted a dramatic title."

"I can't believe you did another one of *me*," I said.

"Yeah, well . . ." He looked super embarrassed, and I was, too.

My face burned. I fanned myself with my hand, shifting my weight, my new sandals pinching my toes.

"Do you want to go . . ." He tilted his head toward the hallway. "Get air? For just a minute? It's pretty hot in here." I could see beads of sweat on his forehead.

"Sure," I said, turning to look around. No one was paying attention to us. "Should we tell someone, or just sneak out?"

"I say we sneak."

chapter 24

IT WAS ALMOST eight; the sun was fading fast as Izzy and I made our way to the side of the library where we'd first eaten lunch together. I didn't want to sit on the ground and mess up the dress Aunt Maureen had bought me, so we lingered near a shadowy tree that looked like it'd been here for generations.

Izzy leaned at first, one foot flat against the trunk, hands in his pockets, but his slick dress shoes made his foot slide back down. Standing up, shifting, he wiped his palms on his pants and then plucked a dandelion from the grass and started twirling it in his fingers.

I laughed quietly.

"I hate dressing up," he said, laughing, too. Something

rustled the branches above us; we both looked and saw a squirrel running away. "Watch out. They'll poop on you."

"Seriously?" I asked, tracking the squirrel's movements.

"For real. My friend got hit twice in one day once," Izzy said, laughing, reliving the memory in his mind. "He was so pissed." He looked back at me, and our eyes locked. "It's cool that your family came."

"I know," I said, nodding enthusiastically. "And they drove! That's more than an entire day and night of driving! Not that they did it all at once. My mom said they stopped in . . ."

Izzy stepped toward me; my words evaporated.

"This could be like the last time I see you, right?" Izzy asked.

"I guess so."

He took another step closer.

He's going to kiss me, I thought.

Izzy's face was inches from my face, closer than any non-relative's had ever been. He looked at my lips and raised his eyebrows in question. "Okay?" he asked.

"Okay," I said, my heart hammering so loudly I was sure he could hear it.

He dropped the dandelion. It tickled the top of my foot when it landed.

In the instant before our lips touched, I worried that my mine would feel like tattered sandpaper. But then I didn't care because his were warm and soft and reminding me of my favorite blanket at home, the pale pink fleece one. He smelled like boy deodorant, punch, and just . . . a really concentrated dose of Izzy. I loved the smell of him.

Our lips pressed together, he wound two fingers around two of mine, an awkward hand hold that was actually just right.

The kiss felt like an hourlong dream but was probably only seven seconds, max. We both pulled apart naturally at the same time, both smiling, me touching the fingers on my free hand to my lips and glancing down at the grass.

"I wish you weren't leaving yet," he said.

I shivered. "Me too," I said automatically.

Part of me wanted to stay to be near Izzy and the others, and part of me felt the pull of home, even though it wouldn't be the same when I got there.

Someone cleared their throat from the path. Izzy dropped my hand, probably thinking it was an adult. Instead, Jackie stood in her tight royal-blue dress with her hands crossed over her chest.

"They're handing out awards," she said flatly. "Karly made me come get you."

She rolled her eyes and went back inside, her blond hair fanning out behind her.

"I wonder if she saw—"

"Who cares?" he asked.

"I don't want her to feel bad," I said.

"You're a nicer person than she is, Tess," Izzy said, taking my hand again and squeezing it. "I'm really glad you spent the summer here. I'm glad I got to hang out with you. I'm also really glad about . . . uh . . . what just happened."

"Me too," I said, feeling the warmth in my cheeks.

"Do you think you'll come back next year?" he asked hopefully.

For kisses like yours, for sure.

"Yeah," I said, an enormous smile on my face. "I think I will."

~

LIKE WE WERE in kindergarten, everyone got an award. Some were for specific art pieces, and some were more about our personalities or behaviors at camp. The adults had been drinking wine and beer all night, so they cheered for every award like us kids were graduating from high school or something. It was ridiculous, but fun, too.

Boy Sam got the award for *Most Helpful*, which I thought was fitting.

Girl Sam was *Most Energetic*.

Axl got *Most Likely to Spill Something*, and the entire room burst into laughter as Axl's mom announced, "Oh yes, he is!" Karly also gave him a certificate for *Best Collage*.

240

Jackie got the award for *Best Abstract Piece.*

"It isn't *that* great," Frankie said too loudly, making me grateful for the noisy applause from tipsy adults.

"Be nice," I said.

"Clapping makes my hands itch," she replied.

"Then stop clapping."

But when Karly gave Jake a certificate that said *Best Photograph*, Frankie clapped anyway, itchy hands or not.

Izzy got *Most Resourceful*; Karly had liked his found art superhero a lot.

Mine came last, after Jasmine and Axl and the sixteen other kids I knew by name but not well enough to talk about over dinner.

"And the last award goes to a camper who's not from around these parts," Karly said into the mic, making a few of the adults chuckle, I wasn't sure why. Frankie elbowed me as if I hadn't already figured out that Karly was talking about me. "We're lucky that Tess Harper was with us this summer all the way from Washington." I heard someone snicker and didn't have to look to know it was Jackie. "And we sincerely hope she'll come back next year."

"Yeah we do!" Girl Sam shouted.

"You'd better come back!" Jasmine chimed in, beaming at me. Axl was nodding next to her, giving me a double thumbs-up. They were such a cute couple.

Were Izzy and I a couple?

I met his gaze, and my cheeks burned hotter than they already had.

"In the meantime," Karly went on, "Tess can remember us with this award for her special piece, which she titled *Lost Girl*. I hope everyone had the chance to see it tonight, because it's magnificent." People clapped, and over them, practically shouting into the mic, Karly said, "Tess, come get your award for the *Best Overall Work*!"

"You won," Frankie said; I couldn't tell if she was impressed.

"I didn't win," I said. "Everyone got awards."

"You got the best one."

Karly was waving me up, and my mom nudged me from behind. I worked my way through the applauding crowd, feeling equally humiliated by the attention and proud of myself for finding my way back to drawing.

I took the certificate that Karly had probably printed at home this morning. My name was spelled *Tess Hatper* and there was clip art of an easel, a cartoon painter, and a cartoon sculptor chiseling the word *CONGRATS*.

"Thank you," I told Karly, loving the certificate and its silliness.

"It's well deserved," she said, beaming. "You're very talented. Keep it up, okay?"

"I will," I said, turning back to where my family was standing, letting them surround me in a monster hug, everyone except Kennedy, who I hadn't seen in hours, and Frankie, of course.

———

AT MIDNIGHT, FRANKIE'S voice cut through the dark bunk room.

"It's driving me crazy," she said.

"Frankie, shh!" I said. "You'll wake up Kennedy." Frankie didn't say anything for a few seconds; we both listened to make sure our cousin's snores were steady.

All of my art from the summer was piled downstairs, but the framed portrait of Colette was propped up on the chair by the window. I could see it in the moonlight.

Hi, friend, I thought, looking at it.

"Stop ignoring me," Frankie said.

I whispered, "Fine. Is it the crickets? Should I close the window?"

"No, I like them."

"You hated them last summer," I said.

"No, I didn't," she said. "I've always liked crickets."

It wasn't worth arguing about, so I asked, "Then what's driving you crazy?"

She rolled over onto her side on the top bunk.

"That girl," Frankie said, lower, but not in a whisper. "The girl with the abstract thingy. I can't figure out where I've seen her, but I *know* I know her."

"I think it was the blog," I whispered. "Just go to sleep, okay? Mom said she's waking us up early to help clean the cabin."

"Why would I go to your art camp blog?" Frankie asked flatly.

"I don't know," I whispered, because why would she? Still, I didn't have an answer to her question. "Let's talk about it in the morning, okay?"

"But it's driving me crazy. I can't sleep."

"Do you want my headphones?" She'd told me she'd broken hers.

"Okay," she said, and I slipped out of bed and got them for her.

Twenty minutes later, she was asleep.

And when my sister was still, so was I.

chapter 25

FRANKIE STOOD NEXT to my bed, staring at me, startling me awake. It wasn't light out, but it wasn't pitch-dark either: it was some early morning hour not meant for my eyelids to be open.

"What's wrong?" I asked. "What time is it?"

"I know where I saw that girl," Frankie said.

"Ohmygod, Frankie, you woke me up for *this*? At . . ." I started to reach for my phone to see what time it was.

"Four freaking forty-five," Kennedy grumbled. "Will you two please shut up already? You're worse than Kane."

Frankie ignored her, I apologized even though I was still mad, and Kennedy ignored me, which made me madder.

Frankie hopped twice, shaking her hands like she couldn't wait to tell me a great secret. I knew there was no way she'd let me go back to sleep until I listened to what she had to say. She looked wired, like she hadn't gone to sleep at all. But I knew she had . . . At least I thought she had.

"Fine, how do you know Jackie?" I whispered.

"From here! At the cabin . . . last year!"

Kennedy growled loudly and put her pillow over her face. She muttered a string of muffled curse words.

"What do you mean? Like, she came to the door or something?" I asked Frankie.

"No, she was outside."

"What was she doing on our property?" I sat up, more awake by the second.

"I don't know," Frankie said.

"But . . . why . . . Where was she? Outside, I mean. Where was she standing?" Getting details from Frankie was sometimes a challenge; I had to ask just the right question in just the right way.

"By the fence." She scratched her face and yawned, clearly growing bored. She'd solved the riddle for herself and now she probably didn't care anymore.

Kennedy certainly didn't either.

"How is this a conversation we need to be having at four o'clock in the morning?" she asked, her words still muffled by the pillow.

"Okay," Frankie said, turning and climbing up the ladder to the top bunk.

"Frankie, wait!" I said, feeling like there was more to the story . . . something I should know. "What was Jackie doing by the fence?"

"How should I know?" Frankie said, scooting under the covers. She yawned again.

Kennedy threw the pillow to the foot of her bed. "There! She doesn't know! Now can you both let me sleep?"

"Fine," I said, lying back, my eyes wide open. The other two settled down and went back to sleep, but I just lay there, staring at the log ceiling, which I could see better by the minute as the night inched toward day.

An hour later, still totally awake, I threw off the covers, put on sweats, and went downstairs. Through the huge window in the living room, I could see a sliver of the sun rising over the mountains.

It was my last day in Pinedale.

I went outside and covered my clothes and any visible skin in bug spray, then went to Colette's rock to watch the sun come up. In the field across the highway, a herd of deer were grazing until the sound of a passing semi scared them away.

I took a picture of the horizontal layers of the sunrise: the black silhouette of land on the bottom, then a goldenrod layer, a coral layer, a maroon layer, a bluish-white layer, and shadowy, rippled clouds on top.

A horse nickered somewhere.

I hugged my knees and rested my chin there, wondering what in the world Jackie could have been doing by our fence last summer. I wished Frankie had been more specific. Then, as if I'd summoned her with my mind, my sister banged out the back door behind me.

"Spray your arms and legs, or the horseflies will attack you," I said, looking over my shoulder at my sister in her dark tank top and shorts.

She shook her head, crunching through the gravel toward me. "They leave me alone." She stopped near the boulder but didn't get on it. Instead, she said, "Climbing."

"Sure, climb up," I said, scooting over into Colette's space.

"No, that girl . . ."

"Jackie," I sighed.

"Yeah, her. She was climbing over the fence." Frankie turned to the right and pointed. "Right there."

"Why would she . . . ?" My words stopped in their tracks as it hit me: Jackie lived next door. My eyes traveled from the low wooden fence to the grand house that was apparently Jackie's, the one that the businessman came out of every day, the one with the silhouette in the window the other night.

"I guess she lives there," Frankie said, matter-of-fact.

"Yeah, I got that," I said.

And then suddenly everything made sense.

It'd been Jackie who'd written in the mirror—and I guess the shower stall, too.

"What a jerk! What is her *problem*?"

Frankie shrugged, still looking at the house. A horsefly hovered near her but didn't land. "Go away, gross thing," she said, and miraculously, it obeyed. She looked back at me. "Colette knew she was a jerk. She talked to her once."

"Colette talked to *Jackie*?" I asked in disbelief.

"If that's what you say her name is."

"Why?"

"Who cares?" Frankie said.

"Did Colette say that she thought Jackie was a jerk?" I asked, realizing I'd started biting my nails, tasting bitter bug spray in my mouth. My heartbeat had picked up, too, and I didn't yet understand why. All I knew was that I needed to know the connection between Colette and Jackie.

"I don't remember what she said about it."

"About what, exactly?" I asked, wanting Frankie to just rewind her brain and start at the beginning. "Tell me all the details."

"I don't remember any details," Frankie said. "I'm bored. I'm going to get a banana." She turned and crunched toward the back door, saying as she went, "Just go ask Jackie if you want to know so bad."

It was all the way light now, but still too early to knock on someone's door.

I'd wait.

⟋

FRANKIE WENT WITH me but stood two steps behind and didn't talk much, lurking like a bodyguard. I bit my nail as we waited for the door to be answered, standing on a huge porch with furniture made to look rustic but that was obviously brand-new.

My stomach flipped when the door opened.

It was Jackie's house, all right, because there in pajamas with donuts all over them, hair in a bird's nest on top of her head, was Jackie. She folded her arms over her big chest and pursed her lips.

"What do you want?" she asked through the screen door, not bothering to open it.

I glanced back at Frankie, who raised her eyebrows at me. After forcing my hands to my sides, I said to Jackie, "I didn't know you lived here."

She rolled her eyes. "Obviously, I do."

"Our cabin is next door," I explained.

"I know," Jackie said.

"Uh . . ." I said, looking at my feet for a second. "My sister"—I gestured toward Frankie—"says you met our friend . . . maybe. She was here with us last summer. Colette?"

"I know who she is," Jackie said, sighing. "She's the girl you drew."

"Yeah," I said, swallowing hard. My throat was dry. A bee zoomed by my head too fast for me to flinch. I looked back at Frankie for reassurance; she gave me one of her rare smiles. Something about having her there made me stronger—and the mean voice in my head had nothing to say. I asked Jackie, "Did you talk to her? Like, last summer?"

"Once or twice," Jackie said, admiring her own nicely painted nails, her arms still crossed. She seemed like she was putting on a brave act. "She asked me to do her a favor."

"What was it?" I asked. She hesitated, like she didn't want to tell me. "Come on, Jackie, she was our best friend. And now she's—"

"Fine," she interrupted. "She asked me to take a picture of her. She said it was some surprise for you guys. She made me text it to her and then she was going to show you when you came back this summer." Hurt flashed into her eyes. "And then, like, I asked if I could join this game you guys were playing, and she said she'd ask you guys, and I never saw her again." She paused, adding, "Whatever. It's not like I wanted to hang out with a diva from Seattle."

"We don't live in Seattle," Frankie corrected her flatly.

"Colette was *not* a diva," I said angrily, clenching my fists.

Jackie shrugged. "Seemed like it." She looked over her shoulder into the house, then stepped closer to the door, like she didn't want anyone inside to hear her. "I told you what you wanted to know. Now leave."

That wasn't good enough for me.

"How can you call Colette a diva? What did she do to you?"

"Besides thinking she and her friends were too good to hang out with me?" Jackie asked back.

"We were just having fun together," I said softly.

"Oh, I know, I heard," Jackie snapped. "All of your stupid games and stupid deep conversations and ghost stories keeping me up—"

"Speaking of that," I interrupted, putting up a hand. Jackie looked down at her toes. I stepped closer to the screen door. "I know you heard the story about William." It wasn't a question; I was certain. "I know what you did."

When Jackie looked up, she had tears in her eyes.

"I've liked him since second grade," she whispered.

It was like I'd had a dormant volcano inside me—now it erupted.

"Are you serious?" I screamed, not caring who heard, whether it was Jackie's parents or the entire state of Wyoming. "You made it seem like our dead best friend was haunting me, scaring me and, worse, like dishonoring her, all because you're . . . just . . . freaking . . . *jealous*?" My face was an inch from her screen door; she backed up. Angry tears streamed down my face. "That is not a normal response! You can't do that to people!"

"It's pretty bad," Frankie reiterated.

"I'm sorry," Jackie said, sobbing. "It went too far."

"You think?" I shouted. "I never did anything to you, and you ruined my summer!"

"Jackie?" someone called from inside her house.

"Tess?" my mom called from our cabin porch. I glanced over at her but didn't answer.

"I honestly can't believe you'd do something like that," I said at a lower volume, but with just as much anger. It felt good to stand up for myself.

"I know," Jackie sobbed.

"You don't even know me!"

"I'm sorry," she said again.

"It's not okay!" I snapped.

"Tess?" my mom said, concerned. "What are you doing?"

She, Aunt Maureen, and Kennedy had all walked over and were standing on our side of the fence in the sagebrush. My mom looked horrified, Aunt Maureen looked worried, and Kennedy looked amused.

"It's all good, Mom," Frankie said. "Tess is standing up to a bully."

"I'm not a bully," Jackie said weakly. "I've never done anything like this before."

"That doesn't make it okay," I said, holding my ground.

A woman with wild white-blond hair and mascara smeared under her eyes, wearing a short, low-cut robe, appeared behind Jackie.

"More than a bully, you're a criminal," I said harshly. Then, louder, I added, "You broke into our house."

"Okay, that's it, I'm coming over," I heard my mom say. As my family started climbing over the fence, Jackie's mom grabbed her arm and spun her around.

"What did you do this time?" Jackie's mom hissed. "I swear, I'm *this close* to sending you to live with your father."

"I didn't do anything," Jackie said. "It's a misunderstanding." She looked at me, her bright blue eyes pleading. "Right, Tess?" To her mom, she said, "This is Tess, from art camp. She's the one who won last night, remember?"

Her mom's blank expression made it seem like she was clueless.

My family was almost to the porch.

"You guys go back," I told them. "Everything's okay. I've got this."

I gave them a look that said I meant it. My mom put her hand on Aunt Maureen's forearm to stop her from walking.

"Are you sure?" Mom asked.

"Yes," Frankie and I said in unison.

"Come on, Ken," Aunt Maureen said to Kennedy, taking her hand.

Kennedy let herself be pulled back toward our cabin, watching me with curious excitement the whole way. Frankie stayed with me, right behind me, literally having my back.

"Sorry for the noise," I said to Jackie's mom, not agreeing with Jackie that it was a misunderstanding—but I think she took it that way.

"Well," Jackie's mom said, pursing her lips like Jackie had earlier. They looked alike. Jackie's mom tightened the belt on her robe and said to her daughter, "Hurry up and shut the door, then. You're letting the air out."

After she'd disappeared into the house, Jackie exhaled like she'd been holding her breath.

"I'm so sorry," she said, looking over her shoulder to make sure her mom wasn't there. It didn't seem like they had a great relationship, and that made me feel a little bad for her.

I still didn't forgive her for what she'd done to me.

"Do you still have the picture you took of Colette?" I asked coldly.

Jackie wiped under her eyes. "I think so."

I told her my number; she put it in her phone. "Send it to me."

And then me and my bodyguard walked away.

I'D ONLY JUST sat down at the kitchen table with the sticky tablecloth and inedible lemon centerpiece when the text from Jackie came through.

She'd attached five pictures, all taken in the same outdoor location. I could imagine Colette telling Jackie to "take another one" as she moved through poses: Colette was serious in two, smiling in two, and making a silly face with her tongue sticking out in one. But in every picture, my friend pointed up at the sky, saying she was number one? That was my first thought.

Zooming in, I realized I was wrong.

It was an illusion picture, which I knew after the photography unit with Karly was really called forced perspective. It was like when Mia's parents took her on vacation to France and she sent us a picture that made it look like she was holding the Eiffel Tower in her palm.

In these, taken on a field on the side of the highway, aiming toward town, Colette's pictures made it look like she was balancing something on the tip of her finger. That's what she wanted us to see.

Then.

And now.

That something was the bridge.

chapter 26

FRANKIE AND I trudged along, cars, minvans, RVs, pickups, and semis zooming by on the two-lane highway to our left, houses set back from the road on our right. Some people had mowed their land like us, but others left the prairie grass long. It made my bare ankles itch, but our mom had made us promise not to walk on the shoulder.

She'd been surprisingly cool about all of it. She hadn't pushed too hard when I didn't give a lot of details about the situation next door. She'd agreed when I asked if we could leave tomorrow instead of today. And when Frankie and I had insisted that we *had* to walk toward town to investigate something, but wouldn't tell her what it was and wouldn't let her come with us, she'd managed to keep her protectiveness in check and let us go.

"Text when you get there," she said.

"Of course," I said at the same time that Frankie replied, "My phone's out of battery."

"And text when you're on your way back."

"We will," I said at the same time that Frankie replied, "She will."

"And put on sunscreen and promise to walk closer to the houses, not on the shoulder."

So, here we were, walking in buggy fields, my shoulder getting crispy where Frankie missed a spot with the spray sunscreen.

According to GPS, the animal crossing was only a mile away from the cabin, so the walk was easy, except for me worrying about a rock kicking up from one of the passing cars and hitting me in the head.

I'll die and never know what Colette was trying to tell me.

Not this again, Mean Me groaned.

Not you again!

"Your face looks weird," Frankie said. The dry grass crackled under our sneakers.

"Thanks." I sighed.

"You make that face a lot."

"I don't do it on purpose," I said. "I was just . . . thinking."

"Worrying, you mean," she said. "I told you . . . you have to schedule your worries."

"I know, but I can't always do it." I put my hand on my shoulder to cover up the part that was getting burned.

"That's weird. It's easy."

"Not everything that's easy for you is easy for me," I said.

"Duh." Frankie twisted a black woven bracelet on her wrist.

"Where'd you get that?"

"Kennedy."

"Just now? When they left?" I asked, eyes on the overpass in the distance. The road was flat and straight, so I could see it as we approached. It sat there, making me shiver in the heat, waiting for us.

Frankie ignored my question. "The clouds are cumulus now, but maybe they'll turn into cumulonimbus clouds later, which are storm clouds." She started talking about tornadoes, and I thought about saying goodbye to my relatives.

After hugging Uncle Bran and Aunt Maureen, I'd pulled Kennedy aside and apologized.

"I can't believe I thought it was you," I said. "That was so stupid."

Kennedy laughed. "Not really," she said. "It's not completely out of character for me, but I wouldn't do that to you," she added quickly. "And I'm sorry, too. I don't . . ." She twisted her face, thinking. "I hope we can hang out again next summer. But let's keep in better touch when we're at home, okay?"

"Okay," I said, hugging her tightly when she stepped closer. We broke away, and she sniffed, tears in her eyes.

"I'll miss you waking me up in the middle of the night."

"I'll miss waking you up."

She got in the minivan with Kane without saying anything else. Through the tinted window, I saw the shadow of her climb to the third row, sit down, and put on headphones.

I went around and opened the slider door on Kane's side, giving him a big hug in his booster seat.

"I'll miss you," I told him, my hands on his squishy knees.

"I'll miss you too, Teth, and I'll think about you every day all the days except when I'm sleeping that's silly," he said, making me laugh and tear up again.

"I'll think about you every time I draw a picture using green pencil," I said. "Or anytime I eat something with ketchup!"

"Eeeeeew!" Kane shrieked. "Ketchup is icky, Teth!"

Laughing, I gave him another quick hug and turned away. "See you."

"Stop ignoring me," Frankie said, cutting into my thoughts.

"Sorry." I didn't try to deny it. "I was just thinking of everyone leaving. It was kinda sad."

"Okay."

"Hey, I'm really sorry again for yelling at you that time," I said. "I hate when I go Angry Tess on you." I almost said she didn't deserve it, but I wasn't so sure about that. Still, I didn't like how I'd yelled. I wished I were better at just talking to my sister instead of either agreeing with everything she said or blowing up at her.

I made a silent vow to work on that.

"Sometimes Angry Tess is good," Frankie said. "Like you slayed standing up for yourself with that girl—"

"Jackie."

"Yeah, that girl." She looked away from me and said, "I know sometimes I do stuff that makes it hard to be nice to me." We walked a few steps in silence. "It's not like I don't know."

"I know," I said softly.

"Anyway."

We walked along in silence for the rest of the way, me thinking about how much I appreciated Frankie standing by me at Jackie's, and her probably wishing for a tornado to hit. Then, eighteen minutes after we'd jumped off the cabin porch, we made it to the fence that kept people off the overpass. It took me a minute, but I figured out how to open the gate.

"Why the heck was Colette obsessed with this thing?" Frankie asked, her hands on her hips, looking up at the animal crossing. "It's just a hill with grass on it."

"It's an overpass."

"Duh, but it looks like a normal hill from the side. What's the big deal?"

"I don't know," I said, the fairies having a party on my spine: they'd invited all their friends. I wrapped my arms around my waist. "I'm freaking out."

"About what?" Frankie asked. "There better not be animal poop up there."

Without another word, she started up.

I felt sick, standing this close to the overpass that had bugged me all summer. I wanted to run back to the cabin, but I didn't because I had to know.

Don't be the wimp you really are, the mean voice said.

"I'm not a wimp," I said aloud, thinking of standing up to Jackie, of telling Izzy I liked him, of coming here in the first place and letting others see my art. "I'm not a wimp!" I said louder.

Frankie looked over her shoulder at me. "I didn't say you were."

Quieter, I said to myself, "I can do this."

I went after Frankie, who'd already made it to the center of the crossing, the highest point. The overpass was low enough to the ground that it felt like the semitrucks wouldn't make it under. There was a wire fence, but I still worried that we'd somehow fall. It was terrifying.

Frankie stood like a superhero, watching the oncoming traffic.

"I low-key love this," she said, adjusting her stance so her feet were wider apart. "If you stand like I am, it's like the cars are driving under your legs."

"Don't fall off!"

"Why would I do that?"

"Just help me look . . ." I turned around and watched the backs of the cars zoom toward town. On the top of the crossing, just like when I'd looked back at it so many times, I saw nothing. It was just like Frankie had said: a grassy hill. There were rocks here and there, some smaller and some . . .

"Frankie! Look!"

The dirt swished as she spun. "Oh," she said, seeing it, too. "It's a decorated rock."

"It's from Colette," I said confidently, taking a step toward it.

"Uh, yeah, I don't think deer use sparkle pink nail polish." She laughed at her own joke.

The rock was about the size of a shoebox, gray and smooth-looking, with three letters painted on top: *T, F,* and *C.*

"That was her favorite color polish," I said, approaching it like it was going to come alive and scare me. "Why did she leave a decorated rock up here?"

"It must be the time capsule," my sister said, following

me. "I heard her talking to Mia about it once when they were in your room and they didn't know I was in mine. Colette said she was going to surprise us."

"Why didn't you tell me that?" I asked, putting my hands up in exasperation.

"I didn't know it was *here*," she said. "How did I know she put a time capsule on a deer bridge in Wyoming?"

That was Frankie, always collecting pieces of things, but not necessarily putting them together until she needed to.

"What?" she asked. "Stop staring at me."

I shook my head and focused on the rock. I bent down and struggled to move it: it was really heavy, which was probably why it hadn't budged in a year. I wondered if it'd already been up here, or if Colette had found it in the field and carried it up. She hadn't had great upper body strength.

I laughed quietly.

"Are you thinking of her trying to carry this thing?" Frankie asked, reading my mind.

I laughed harder, nodding. "Yeah."

She laughed, too, then bent down and helped me shove the rock to the side. Underneath was an envelope with plastic wrap taped to the outside.

"I wouldn't call that a time capsule," Frankie said, scratching her head, then blowing her bangs out of her eyes. "It should be a box."

"Are you seriously correcting our dead best friend?" I asked.

"I'm just saying." She shrugged.

Frankie and I both sat down on the ground. I hoped no antelope would suddenly need to cross the street right now—or moose. Weren't they mean? I didn't know, but I looked around just to make sure I couldn't see any herds coming. The fields were clear.

"Rip it," Frankie bossed.

"I'm trying," I said, pulling at the plastic. "She must have used a whole roll of that really strong kind of tape."

Cars zoomed below us, making my ears vibrate as they went by. Finally, I got the package open.

Frankie leaned close, peering in. "What is it?"

"Looks like . . ." I felt inside, pulling out two sheets of paper with our names on them. "Letters."

"*Letters?*" Frankie asked, disappointed. "That's not a time capsule! That's just . . . mail!"

I felt like I could hear Colette laughing with me. I realized that there was something comforting in how Frankie still treated Colette after her death just like she'd treated her when she was alive.

Frankie took her letter and stood up. "This is boring. Let's go."

"Aren't you going to read it?" I asked, surprised.

"Later," she said before walking down the side of the overpass toward the gate. I didn't know for sure but wondered if Frankie wanted to read the letter from Colette in private, in case it made her emotional. She didn't usually cry in front of other people.

I realized I wanted to read mine in private, too. The letter in my hands was for me and me alone, written by a girl who'd probably thought she'd be sitting next to me when I opened it. Gently touching the edge of the paper, I pictured Colette's perfect handwriting inside, the curls and shapes of it forming sentences and secrets and predictions and her purposely ridiculous punctuation, all of it meant just for me. I didn't want even the horseflies reading over my shoulder.

I stayed on the overpass for a few moments longer, until Frankie yelled at me to hurry up because she was hungry and had to pee. But sitting there, cross-legged over the two-lane highway, land stretching out forever, I was aware of being right where Colette had been last year.

I put my hand over my heart, knowing.

None of the rest had been real: Jackie and the messages, William and the scarf. But maybe this one was. Maybe, this whole time, from wherever she was now, Colette had just wanted to give me a letter.

"I love you," I told her, hoping she could hear.

I stood up, and a minivan zoomed under, kind of like the

one I'd been riding in all summer, but a different color. I wondered where it was going. I wondered if someone inside was looking back at me.

Just before I left the animal bridge, I realized something.

Sometime between standing in the field and now, the fairies had gone away.

epilogue

TEN MONTHS LATER, Frankie and I sat across from each other at our favorite spot, sharing a colossal basket of Tater Tots with every sauce: sriracha, ranch, honey mustard, barbecue, and Kane's least favorite, ketchup. We both had soda: hers was orange, and mine was root beer. We'd shared Tater Tots together here once a week since last summer, but this would be the last for a while since tomorrow I'd leave for Wyoming.

I couldn't believe it was already here.

"What if Jackie's back at camp?" Frankie asked, talking with her mouth full.

"She will be," I said. "Sam told me." Girl Sam and I had gotten close this year; I was excited to hang out with her this summer.

"Don't let Jackie be mean to you," Frankie said.

"Oh, I won't," I promised, knowing that Jackie would probably just ignore me, like I'd ignore her. Thankfully, Izzy had told me she'd moved on and was dating some guy from their school, baking *him* birthday cakes now.

"You'd better not forgive her."

I thought about that. "I don't forgive her yet, but I don't hate her."

"You don't hate anyone," Frankie said.

I shrugged with one shoulder, thinking she was right, thinking of what our mom always said, that hating people took too much energy.

Mom and I had talked a lot more over the school year, about stuff like that but other things, too, like what was really going on in my head a lot of the time. She'd made an effort to spend time with just me, and I felt like she understood me better now. Maybe I understood her better, too— well, except about annoying parent stuff like my too-early curfew and screen time limits.

I looked down at my hands and felt proud of myself: my fingernails weren't long, but they all had white parts above the pink, and the cuticles around them didn't look like hell.

The medicine I'd been taking had helped, and so had my therapist. She'd taught me how to question my negative thoughts and to challenge that mean voice in my head. She'd taught me that it was like a bully that I had to stand up to. After going head-to-head with Jackie, it'd gotten easier to go head-to-head with myself.

I was meditating.

I was eating a lot of ice cream.

I was hanging out with my sometimes frustrating but always interesting sister, and even making some new friends at school.

I was laughing.

I was spending a lot of time texting and talking to Izzy, who I couldn't wait to see.

And I was drawing.

"Are you sad you're not going to Wyoming?" I asked Frankie, pulling hair out of my mouth. I'd cut it to my shoulders and my mom had let me put a streak of blue in the front, which made me feel powerful.

"No way," Frankie answered. "The crickets keep me up all night! I hate them!"

"I thought you loved them," I said, distinctly remembering our conversation about that last year.

"I've never loved them!" Frankie said, looking at me like I was the craziest person on Earth, stuffing more Tater Tots into her mouth. "You're the worst listener."

The crickets weren't a big deal, but I'd gotten better about talking to Frankie about things that *were* a big deal to me, calling her on rude comments instead of just letting everything slide because I didn't want to start drama.

"That wasn't nice," I pointed out. "I try hard to be a good listener."

A ladybug landed on my leg; I watched it walk across my thigh before it took off, carried away on tiny wings. Frankie didn't say anything.

"Did you hear me?" I asked. "I don't think I'm a bad listener. In fact—"

"Okay, okay," she interrupted. "I don't mean always. I just meant you didn't listen to me about the crickets. Don't start telling me I made your paper heart wrinkly or whatever again."

"Then be more careful with what you say."

"Fine." She didn't sound mad.

"Hey, I'm going to miss you."

"You'll be too busy kissing Izzy to miss me," Frankie teased.

"Shut up." I threw a Tot at her, and she dodged it, looking at me sternly.

"Sorry," I said, shifting my legs; they were falling asleep. "Honestly, I'm worried about all that stuff."

"Kissing's no big deal," Frankie said, half shrugging. I couldn't believe she'd let her boyfriend, Kai, get close enough to her face to kiss her, but she had. "And besides, you've already done it!"

The alarm went off on my phone; I needed to finish packing. "We have to go," I told my sister, sad that it'd be another six weeks until we could have our Tater Tot date again.

Frankie stood up, brushing the dirt off her shorts. She always made such a mess. "Remember to just schedule your kissing worries for the middle of the night," she said. "That's what I do."

"Cheat the system," we said in unison.

I brushed the dirt off the back of my shorts, too, and leaned over to grab our trash. "Hey, who told you to do that, anyway?" I asked, stepping on a stray napkin that was trying to escape on the breeze. "The thing about scheduling worries."

"I told you already a million times." Frankie wiped ranch dressing from her wrist onto her shorts.

She definitely hadn't.

"Tell me again, then."

Frankie rolled her eyes and patted the marble next to her. "She did."

I looked at Colette's tombstone, at the deep engraved letters of her name, her birthdate, and the day she died— now more than a whole year ago. The year had gone by fast and slow at the same time.

"Of course she did," I said, thinking of how much Colette had been there for my sister. How much she'd been there for me. Quieter, I repeated, "Of course."

Two days later, in a town I now thought of as my second home, I stood like a superhero on the animal overpass, the blue streak in my hair blowing wild in the Wyoming wind. Cars and trucks zoomed by on the two-lane highway below and an aggressive horsefly hovered close, but I wasn't afraid.

I looked over my shoulder and waved at the boy waiting by the gate, the one who'd known to let me come up alone and who I'd have to get on tiptoes to kiss when I was done, he'd grown so tall this year.

I think I love you, Izzy, I thought, smiling, my mean voice silent.

I walked over and lifted one side of the heavy rock with *T, F,* and *C* painted in sparkle pink nail polish on top, just enough to slide a letter wrapped in plastic underneath before dropping the rock back to the ground.

The letter was written by a girl who never thought she'd lose her best friend but had, a girl who'd had a hard time picking up the pieces afterward—but who was doing a little better every day now.

I pictured my imperfect handwriting inside, the curls and shapes of it forming sentences and secrets I needed to share with my best friend, predictions about a future

I'd have without her—but with her, too, since she would always—always—be in my heart.

The letter was meant just for Colette, and I hoped, somehow, some way, she'd read it in private, with not even a horsefly looking over her shoulder.

Turn the page for a sneak peek of the companion novel from Frankie's perspective

chapter 1

Fact: In some parts of the country,
middle schools have built-in tornado shelters.

COLETTE WENT MISSING on the second Friday in April, almost at the end of seventh grade. It was seven and a half years after the tornado in kindergarten, and Colette and I hadn't been friends anymore for two months.

Before any of us knew she was missing, it was a normal morning. My mom appeared in my doorway at six thirty. Opening my eyes and seeing a person in the doorway made my heart jump.

"I hate it when you do that!" I complained.

"Good morning, Frankie," Mom said in a soothing voice. "Time to get ready for school."

I closed my eyes again.

I'd had trouble falling asleep the night before because I'd been playing something over in my head and when I'm thinking too much at bedtime, my brain doesn't turn off and go to sleep. Plus, I'd forgotten to take the vitamin that helps me sleep. And then I'd woken up twice during the night for no reason, once at two thirty and once at five. It's hard for me to get back to sleep when that happens. Adding it all together, I'd probably had about four hours of sleep.

I rubbed my eyes with my fists, then scooted deeper under the covers, wishing my mom would go away. But I could still smell the scents she'd brought in with her: nice shampoo and disgusting coffee. I pictured a cartoon drawing of coffee-smell pouncing on a cartoon drawing of nice-shampoo-smell. The nice-shampoo-smell fought back and shoved the coffee-smell off, then . . .

"Are you awake, Frankie?" my mom said.

I am now.

Lately, I'd been concentrating on using manners, so I focused on not yelling that I wanted her to leave so I could wake up in peace. *Do not yell,* I told myself, my voice loud in my head. *Do not tell her to get out. Make your voice match hers.*

I opened my eyes and looked at her sideways because I was on my side.

"Hi," I groaned, my tired, grumpy, scratchy voice not sounding like hers at all. She ignored it.

"It's Friday!" Mom said. "Or, since it's your early-release day, should I say, Fri-*yay*?"

We got out of school at 11:25 a.m. on Fridays, so we were

2

only there for three hours and five minutes, or three class periods—and one of them was homeroom—unless you were an overachiever who'd chosen to take zero period. Zero period is the optional period *before* homeroom and it's way too early for me.

"Uh-huh," I growled, rolling away and pulling the covers over my shoulder. "I'm awake, you can leave now."

"You know the rule," Mom said. "I can't leave until you're upright."

That is the stupidest rule ever! I shouted in my head. It was almost painful not to say it out loud, but I thought about manners and counted to ten and managed not to yell. I threw off my covers and got out of bed, hunched forward, my fists clenched, frowning. But upright.

"There," I said.

"Thank you," my mom said, which bugged me.

I guess I should say right now that I love my mom, so you don't get the wrong idea. She's not mean or anything. I just . . . Things bother me really easily. Or they don't bother me at all. I tend to have extreme feelings one way or the other, not usually in the middle. Maybe that's why I'm sometimes unhappy. I don't know. Anyway.

When my mom finally left, I put on my softest skinny jeans, the ones that I wore at least twice a week. Today, I noticed the seams digging against the sides of my thighs and I hated it, so I changed into a different pair. I pulled on my black hoodie with the thumbholes, testing out the feeling of that for a second, deciding it was okay. The seams of the new pants bugged me, too, so I changed into leggings. They had a hole in the knee but felt okay. I stuck my long fingernail in the hole and made it bigger.

I shoved my unfinished homework into my backpack, then went to brush my teeth. In the mirror, a girl with messy, chin-length hair and too-long bangs, bloodshot brown eyes with dark circles under them, and cracked lips stared back at me. I looked down at my toothbrush: there was a hair on it. I threw it away and leaned over to get a new one out of the cabinet. While I was searching, I found a headband I used to wear all the time when I was younger. I'd never wear it now, but I tried it on, wishing I could text a picture of myself to Colette because I looked hilarious, but I couldn't because we weren't friends anymore. I left the bathroom, dropping the headband on the floor.

I pulled my hood up over my bedhead. From the mini-fridge in my room, I got out the milk, then made myself a bowl of the single brand of cereal I like in the world. I checked my TwisterLvr feed and read about an EF2-category tornado that'd happened in Birmingham, Alabama, the night before. I didn't check my other social media anymore because I didn't want to see all the pictures of Colette and her other friends.

I got my jacket and left. I wanted to ride my favorite

yellow beach cruiser to school, but it wasn't where it was supposed to be, so I had to walk. Only a minute or two into the walk, my phone buzzed in my pocket.

Do you have your backpack?

I turned around to get it. At the door, Mom held out the pack in one hand and a protein bar in the other. Her dark hair was in a tight bun that looked uncomfortable. I patted the top of my head.

"Don't forget to eat it, please."

"I won't," I said, turning to leave again. She was always reminding me to eat. She didn't remind other people to eat—just me. I guess maybe I needed to be reminded sometimes, but it was still annoying.

"I don't want you to get hangry," she said.

Did you know that the word *hangry* is officially in the dictionary now? It is. I looked it up.

"I'm old enough to know when I need to eat," I complained.

"Yes, at thirteen, you *are* old enough," she said in a way that made me think she was trying to make a point. "Did you brush your teeth?"

"Yes," I said, not totally sure whether I had or not. "Bye."

"Have a great day, Frankie! I love you!"

I made a sound and left again, taking the beach path so I could shout into the wind if I felt like it. I didn't this morning, but I like having options. I like choosing what I get to do because it feels like people are always bossing me around. The only thing is, the beach path takes longer than just walking straight to school. It's like turning the route into an obtuse triangle instead of a line from point A to point B.

Do you know what that is? It's geometry, which I like.

I was late to school so often that the hall monitor didn't blink. I left some books and the uneaten protein bar in my locker, which I don't share with anyone because I don't like when their books touch mine, and left a trail of sand like bread crumbs as I walked down the carpeted hallway to homeroom. The bell rang when I was about halfway to class, and Ms. Garrett didn't say anything when I walked in.

All the other kids were already at their desks, most of them socializing. That's a thing I'm not good at, probably because I don't like *chitchat*—the word itself or the act of doing it.

I sat down at my own private desk island by the window and checked my TwisterLvr account again. Nothing new had happened since the last time I'd checked, which was disappointing.

"Phones away or they're mine," Ms. Garrett said. Some people groaned, but everyone made their phones disappear. Not literally: I don't go to Hogwarts.

Ms. Garrett kept talking: "Let's all work on something productive. That means you too, Anna and Daphne. Marcus! Settle down now."

The room got quiet. Everyone took out homework, because first period is homeroom and that's what you do. I opened *Call of the Wild*, which is about a dog named Buck who lives in the freezing Yukon. Sometimes I specifically don't like books that other people tell me to read, but I liked that one even though reading it wasn't my idea.

This lady—this specialist who was always checking in with me at school—popped her head into the room. Her name is Ms. Faust and she's fine, I guess, except no one else has weird ladies checking up on them, so I pretended not to notice her and eventually she left. Ms. Faust was assigned to me or whatever, so it was her job to check in, but I didn't care. I didn't want her anywhere near me.

I was several chapters into my book when Ms. Garrett put her bony hand on my shoulder, startling me. I cringed and pulled away from her, biting my tongue so I wouldn't say anything she'd think was rude. I didn't want her to call my mom. I touched my opposite shoulder to even myself out, looking down at my notebook and noticing that I'd drawn a few tiny tornadoes while I'd been reading.

"Sorry, Frances," she said, looking embarrassed.

"My name is Frankie," I snapped accidentally. Thankfully, she let it go.

"Again, I apologize. I know you don't like when people touch you, but you didn't answer when I said your name." I strained my neck looking up at her because Ms. Garrett is skyscraper tall (not literally, of course). She kept talking. "Uh, I notice that you're reading your book for English, which is great, but I wanted to make sure you've finished your math homework. We only have a few minutes left in the period and Mr. Hubble asked me to check with you. He said that yesterday, you—"

"It's in my backpack," I interrupted, which wasn't a lie. It *was* in my backpack. It was also unfinished.

"I see," Ms. Garrett said. She tilted her head to the side like my dog does sometimes.

Behind Ms. Garrett, across the room in the regular rows, several kids were watching us. Tess smiled at me with her mouth but not her eyes, a halfway smile, which was confusing; Kai smiled at me with his mouth *and* his eyes, an all-the-way smile, which was confusing in a different way; and Mia didn't smile, just stared, which wasn't confusing in the least. I frowned at all of them and they went back to their classwork.

Ms. Garrett opened her mouth to say something else— maybe to ask to see my homework—but the announcement bell chimed, and the office lady started talking. That was unexpected, because it wasn't announcement day, which is Tuesday. And if we *had* had announcements, they would have been at the beginning of the period, not the end.

"Attention, students and staff," the office lady said. "Please proceed immediately in an orderly fashion to the auditorium for an address from Principal Golden. Thank you."

Ms. Garrett looked at me blankly for a few seconds like she was stunned, but then she told everyone to get up and move toward the auditorium. Kai smiled at me all-the-way again as he left the classroom with his friends. Confused by how I felt about that, I waited until everyone else left, too, and then went into the hall.

I watched Kai walk like he was going to wobble over, laughing so hard his eyes got watery as his friend Dillon told a story about some try-hard tourist who had wiped out at the skate park. Kai had on dark blue skate pants with cargo pockets and checkerboard slip-on sneakers and his shiny black hair looked especially interesting, like he'd been blasted by a huge gust of wind from behind and his hair had gotten stuck. I could see a scab on the back of his arm above his left elbow, which grossed me out.

Their conversation got quieter, then Dillon turned around and looked at me, so I stopped watching Kai and stared at the wall instead.

You should know that most people think Ocean View Middle School looks incredibly strange. About five years ago, when the old school was getting run-down, instead of wrecking it and building something new, they just added on. The front part with the offices, cafeteria, and math and English halls is clean and bright, but the back part with the auditorium and shop and music rooms is dark and smells like old sneakers.

I like to run my hands along walls when I walk because I don't like being surrounded by the other kids since they sometimes accidentally bump me. That's what I was doing when Tess appeared next to me.

Tall and skinny, not as tall as Ms. Garrett, though, she walked sort of bent in on herself like she was trying to be shorter. Her smooth, dark hair was parted on the side, so she had to tuck the hair-curtain behind her right ear to make eye contact. Eye contact made me uncomfortable.

"Did you get in trouble?" she asked quietly, raising her perfectly neat eyebrows. I stared at them: Eyebrows are really weird, actually. They never exactly match. There's always . . .

"Frankie?"

"Huh?"

"I asked if you got in trouble?" Tess repeated.

"For what?"

"For not doing your homework?" She practically whispered it. Tess talked super-quietly, like she didn't want anyone to hear her. I barely could.

"I did my homework," I said, which wasn't a lie. I'd done

some of my homework. And it wasn't really her business in the first place. But I managed not to tell her that. Despite getting hungrier by the second, I was doing okay at manners so far today. I mean, except when I'd snapped at my teacher. But since she hadn't gotten mad, it didn't count.

"Oh, okay," Tess said. "Sorry."

Mia nudged Tess and told her to look at something on her social feed and Tess did and they both giggled—Mia loudly and Tess softly—and I was happy not to be asked any more questions about my homework.

In the auditorium, I followed Tess and Mia down the aisle. Tess was half a head taller than Mia and Mia's butt was half a cheek bigger than Tess's. Tess walked like a normal teenager in her skinny jeans and gray T-shirt with an open sweater that looked like a blanket over it. Mia swayed her hips back and forth in her flowy jumpsuit, making her long, curly blond hair sway, too. They picked a row and I sat behind them on the end by the aisle. I looked around, not seeing where Kai was sitting.

I did notice Ms. Faust smiling at me encouragingly from where she was leaning against the far wall. I wished she'd look at someone else.

"Move over," a mean kid named Alex said, staring down at me. He was always yelling at people—a few times even teachers. I may have big emotions, but not like Alex. "Make room for other people."

"I was here first," I said, my need to sit on the aisle out-weighing my desire not to get yelled at by Alex. I really don't like being surrounded. "Here," I said, moving my knees to the left so he could squeeze through.

"Whatever," Alex said, shaking his head and stepping on my foot as he shoved past me.

"Ouch!" I said loudly. He rolled his eyes and didn't apologize. I folded my arms over my chest and slumped down in my chair.

It took a while for all 323 students to sit down. Well, 322 today, but we didn't know that yet. The room felt like being on a beach when an electrical storm is coming, like you could get zapped any minute. That's figurative language—similes and metaphors and stuff. I'm trying to use it more instead of being so literal all the time because people laugh at you when you're literal.

Onstage, Principal Golden held up a hand with her middle and ring finger touching her thumb, the pointer and pinkie sticking straight up: the Quiet Coyote.

"So lame," I heard Alex say loudly. Principal Golden looked right at him in a way I wouldn't want to be looked at by the principal, and he didn't say anything else.

Principal Golden sniffed loudly into the microphone.

"Something has happened," she said, her *p*'s making irritating popping sounds in the mic. "This morning, there has been an incident. We're not sure of the details, but one of our Ocean View students is missing."

I heard the buzzing of the microphone for a couple of seconds before the entire auditorium broke out in whispers.

"Did she say missing?"

"I wonder who it is?"

"What do you think happened?"

My mind started ping-ponging from the idea of a missing student to the missing-kid posters on the bulletin board at I Scream for Ice Cream, where my biological father made me and my sister go when he visited last year even though it was the middle of winter and pouring rain and my sister is lactose intolerant. I shook my head to tune back in to what Principal Golden was saying.

" . . . investigating and we don't know anything more at this time. The police are searching the school and want to speak to select students. Rather than further disrupting this already short school day, the administration has decided to cancel class for the rest of the day. If you ride the bus, please see Mrs. Taylor in the office for instructions on . . ."

Everyone got up at once and started talking except me: I stayed in my seat, waiting for the auditorium to thin out. My row had to exit from the other side because I was blocking my end: even mean Alex went the other way, and I was glad because I didn't want my foot trampled again.

It was 9:40 and I was supposed to be starting second period, English, but instead I was going to go home. My stomach rolled with the weird feeling of change. Change is my enemy.

"She's not answering her phone."

I looked over to see Tess and Mia huddled together in the aisle, whispering to each other. "When's the last time you talked to her?"

"Last night before dinner," Mia said, spinning the ring on her middle finger. "She wasn't in zero period. I thought she slept in."

"That's not like her, though," Tess said, chewing her lip. "Her bag's not in our locker." I leaned forward so I could hear Tess better, wondering if it bugged her that Mia's curls were touching her hand. I brushed my own hand like they'd been touching mine. "Is she home sick?"

They looked at each other, both with big eyes that reminded me of a certain comic book cat, Mia's blue like a sunny day and Tess's green-gray like a cloudy one. Maybe they felt me watching them because they both looked at me at the same time.

"Have you talked to Colette?" Tess asked in her tentative voice.

"Of course I've talked to Colette," I said.

"I mean *recently*," Tess clarified. "Like, did you talk to

Colette yesterday?" Now she was pulling on the lip she'd been biting. It was distracting: I wished she'd leave her lip alone.

"No," I said, just to say something. *No* is an easy response for me.

"This is serious," Mia said, leaning forward like my therapist did sometimes. She lowered her voice. "What if it's her?"

"What if what's her?" I asked.

Mia sighed loudly. "Why are you always so spacey?"

Tess gave her a look, then explained, "Frankie, what we're asking is: What if the missing student is *Colette*?"

I stared at her without saying anything because that idea really didn't make sense to me—since I obviously didn't know at the time that the missing student *was* Colette and since I'd been mostly thinking that it felt strange being told to go home when I'd just gotten to school. This was not my normal routine.

"Come on," Mia said, pulling on Tess's arm, "let's go see if the teachers need help."

acknowledgments

PAPER HEART WOULD not have happened without my long-time agent, Dan Lazar, and brilliant editor Stacey Barney. Thank you both for your encouragement, humor, and grace—especially during the nightmare year that was 2020. A huge thank-you, too, to Cecilia de la Campa and Torie Doherty-Munro at Writers House, and Caitlin Tutterow, Eileen Savage, Vanessa DeJesús, and the entire marketing team at G. P. Putnam's Sons. Mad love forever times infinity to Jen Klonsky.

I'd also like to thank my home state of Wyoming and the town of Pinedale for being such a beautiful backdrop for this story. Reader, I hope you enjoyed getting to know a part of the country that is incredibly special to me.

Thank you to family and friends near and far for your

ongoing support. J, C, and L, you are my whole heart. Grandma and Grandpa, thank you for letting me borrow the cabin for a few hundred pages. Even more than the other books, I wish you could have read this one.

Thank you, always, to my readers. And to the teachers and librarians—you are superheroes. Thank you for your dedication to the communities you serve.

Finally, you with the Mean Brain, thank you for raising your hand when you need help. Thank you for your perseverance and hanging in through hard things. Thank you for managing not to listen sometimes. You are so much stronger than you know.